A DANGEROUS SECRET

Government of South Australia

The creation and development of this series was made possible through the Carclew Fellowship, awarded by Arts SA.

Random House Australia Pty Ltd
20 Alfred Street, Milsons Point, NSW 2061
http://www.randomhouse.com.au

Sydney New York Toronto
London Auckland Johannesburg
and agencies throughout the world

National Library of Australia
Cataloguing-in-Publication Entry

Bone, Ian, 1956– .
  A dangerous secret.

For children.
ISBN 1 74051 884 5.

  I. Murphy, Jobi. II. Title. (Series : Bone, Ian, 1956–
Vidz ; bk. 1).

A823.3

Cover design by Mathematics
Text design by Jobi Murphy
Typeset by Asset Typesetting Pty Ltd
Printed and bound by Griffin Press, Netley, South Australia

VIDZ #1

A DANGEROUS SECRET

IAN BONE WITH STORYBOARDS BY JOBI MURPHY

RANDOM HOUSE AUSTRALIA

Scene one

Fade in ...

Not another hairball! What was wrong with Aunt Jenny? Hamish Wajda stood in his auntie's bathroom staring at a humungous ball of hair. It rolled about playfully in the sink, blown by the breeze from the window. Tiny flakes of dandruff fell off and drifted onto the porcelain. Hamish zoomed in on the hairball as if he had a camera. Close-up. *So much hair!* Extreme close-up. *And all hers!* YUK! Something had to be done. The Lone Avenger couldn't allow such a travesty to exist. It must be destroyed. NOW!

It's huge ... horrible!

The Lone Avenger lunges at the hairball.

They struggle like wild animals!

 Hamish picked up the hairball between his fingernails and dropped it into the bin. He smiled as he thought about the Lone Avenger. *Coming soon! The Attack of the Killer Hairball!* Somehow he didn't think they'd be lining up at cinemas to see that one. *The Lone Avenger* had been the title of the short video he'd made to get into Capra Video High School. It starred his dad as the evil Doctor Bender, and himself as ... you guessed it. Hamish had worked so hard making that vid, shooting for hours after school, editing on weekends, using every spare minute of his day.

From the moment he'd heard about Capra Video High School, he knew it was the place for him. A high school with normal lessons that also taught you how to script, shoot and edit professional videos — heaven! He wanted to get into Capra so badly. Which meant making the best audition video. Writing the script wasn't too hard — he'd been writing scripts ever since he knew how to hold a pencil. The stories he wrote at his old school usually sounded and looked like films rather than something from a book. In the end his teachers gave up on trying to make him write stories their way.

Getting hold of a good camera had been a bit of a problem. Hamish owned an old VHS clunker that he'd saved up to buy second-hand, but he needed digital quality for his audition piece. There weren't that many digital cameras in the town of Barnsborough, where he lived, mainly because there weren't that many people. In the end his dad put an ad in the local newspaper, and three people called offering to lend Hamish their digital camcorders. Then there was the filming ...

Hamish sighed as he pulled out his toothbrush from the bathroom cabinet. Casting his dad as the evil Doctor Bender had seemed like a good idea at the time. Hamish's father was a huge man who claimed that his Polish great-grandfather had been a giant. He sold farm machinery during the day, and had a crushing handshake that could make grown men cry. With the right make-up and costume, he looked perfect as Doctor Bender. Trouble was, he sounded awful. Doctor Bender was supposed to laugh maniacally and say evil things, but Hamish's dad made the lines from the script sound like a weather report.

'Come on, Dad,' Hamish would say during the shooting. 'You're evil. You want to take over the world. How does that make you feel?'

'Well,' his father would drawl, 'to tell you the truth, right now I feel like I need to go do a pee ...'

To solve the problem, Hamish had made the character of Doctor Evil a mute who had lost his tongue in a previous fight with the Lone Avenger. And it worked. The board at Capra liked the vid so much that they let him into the school. The day he received the letter had been the best day of Hamish's life. His mum had hugged him and said she was so proud of him. And his dad had said how much they'd miss him ... That's when it had really hit Hamish. Going to Capra meant moving to the city.

He rinsed his mouth out and spat into the sink, running the water round the basin to clean up. He'd been at Capra a few weeks now, and he was quickly realising that even heaven can be hard work. It wasn't so much the lessons, or the extra lectures on film history, that tired him out, it was trying to deal with so many new people all at once. And then there was his new home.

Hamish glanced down at the hairball in the bin. Living with Aunt Jenny was going to take some getting used to. She was a nice person, but she was busy with her job, so cleaning up wasn't a huge priority. Which was amazing considering she was Hamish's mother's sister, and Hamish had never known a more tidy person than his mum.

'Maybe Aunt Jenny was secretly raised by wolves,' he muttered as he put his toothbrush back. He played around with the image of the wolves and his auntie, imagining a scene where the wolves take the baby Jenny in and lick her clean, but she just rubs dirt all over herself again. Then the mother wolf shows the baby how to stack her bones neatly, but Jenny throws them around the den. The mother wolf cuffs her, Jenny cuffs the wolf back. Baby Jenny grows, and the mess grows with her. Perhaps one of those speeded-up scenes, showing the junk piling up, reaching the ceiling ...

A knock at the bathroom door snapped Hamish back to reality.

'Will you be long, Hame?'

He hated people calling him 'Hame', but made an exception with his auntie. She was always warm and friendly, and if it hadn't been for her and her flat he would never have been able to go to Capra.

'You can come in,' called Hamish.

'Off to bed?' said Aunt Jenny, walking in with a hairbrush in her hand. Hamish couldn't help but notice that she was picking large clumps of hair from the brush.

'Um ... er ... maybe,' he replied, distracted by the fine strands of hair that fell to the floor.

'I might turn in too,' said Aunt Jenny, yawning for effect. She pulled the remaining hair from the brush and rolled it around in her fingers. 'How's things at school?' she added. 'You never talk about it much.'

'Mm?' said Hamish, hoping she'd do the right thing and drop the hairball into the bin. 'It's still very new at my school.'

'Well, any time you want to bring a friend over,' said Aunt Jenny. 'It's fine by me.'

'Okay,' said Hamish. The truth was, he didn't have any friends at Capra. Everyone seemed to know each other already, and tight little groups had been formed. He told himself he didn't mind. He was there for the video making, not the social life.

Aunt Jenny took a step towards the bin. 'You haven't been cleaning up in here, have you?' she asked, finally dropping the ball of hair.

'No!' said Hamish, a little too loudly. He watched in horror as the hair fell gracefully towards the bin, bounced off the side and landed on the floor in slow motion. He could even hear a sound-effect 'thump' as it hit the tiled floor.

Aunt Jenny nodded. 'That's good. You always were a tidy boy. I remember you used to spend more time arranging your toys than actually *playing* with them.' She smiled, then left the bathroom.

The hairball stayed behind.

Hamish stared at the horror on the floor. It was calling to him. 'Pick me up, if you dare!' He stepped right over it.

'Bring a friend over?' muttered Hamish as he shut his bedroom door. 'And do what? Play "Roll the hairball"?'

He gave a little shudder and sat on his bed. The giant teddy bear his father had given him as a going away present fell forward onto its nose.

'Come on, Hitchcock,' said Hamish, straightening the bear. 'Can't have you falling over like a drunk.' At first Hamish had been totally embarrassed by his father's present, until his dad had explained that the bear had belonged to him when he was a boy in boarding school. So Hamish had renamed the bear 'Hitchcock', after his favourite film director, and had even grown fond of him over the past couple of weeks. Having set Hitchcock upright, Hamish grabbed his homework to put into his school bag.

He'd had to write an essay entitled: 'What movies mean to me'. A fairly simple topic because movies meant *everything* to him. Ever since he was out of nappies he'd loved going to the cinema to see a new movie. He'd become totally involved in the characters that flickered on the big screen, living their lives with them. He never wanted a movie to end. After everyone had left the cinema, he'd still be sitting in his seat running through the story in his mind. His parents practically had to drag him out of the place. The world looked so flat and dull outside on the main street of Barnsborough. It always seemed mean that everyone expected him to live an ordinary life when he could be inside that darkened cinema living out the most amazing adventures.

How did he put all that into an essay? He started with the line: 'Sometimes when I watch a good movie I feel like I belong there more than I belong in my own life.' Which wasn't a bad beginning. A bit embarrassing, but it was only meant to be read by a teacher. What Hamish hadn't counted on was nosy classmates with sticky fingers.

He sighed as he remembered what had happened that morning. It ran through his mind like a scene from a movie. He could see it playing, he could even imagine what it looked like as a movie script. Pity he couldn't cut it out and throw it away.

2

Scene two

The camera opens on a shot of HAMISH eating his
lunch in the outside tables area at Capra. He is alone.
His essay is in front of him, and Hamish is eating his
sandwich with one hand and making notes on the page
with the other. A group of students come out of the
building, and a tall girl from his year, KAZ, sits on the
table-top opposite Hamish. Everyone seems to like Kaz.
As if to prove this, several of the other students follow
her and occupy the seats around Hamish. He looks up
at the group, then concentrates on his essay.

> KAZ
>
> Oh, man. If I don't get some money soon I'm
> gonna be fried. I owe everyone.

STUDENT 1
You don't owe me money … yet.

The group laugh loudly. See Hamish in a closer shot. He'd like to join in, but obviously feels shy with these confident students. A dishevelled-looking boy, BO, opens a small jar of strawberry jam and begins to spread the jam onto a roll, using his fingers. Hamish stares at this, totally transfixed. Bo grins at him.

BO
Hey, don't worry. They're my fingers, so they're my germs.

HAMISH
It's still disgusting …

Kaz looks at Hamish, raising her eyebrows at what he's said. She leans forward.

KAZ
Why don't you lighten up a little?

BO
Yeah, man. You're in Capra High …

KAZ
This place is so cool.

BO
You always look like you're having a bad time.

Hamish is taken aback by this attack. He wants to defend himself, but can't get a word in. He is about to say something, when Bo grabs his essay.

> BO
> What's this?

Hamish jumps up to stop him.

> HAMISH
> Hey, leave that!

> STUDENT 2
> Whoo, sensitive ...

Bo reads Hamish's essay out loud.

> BO
> 'When I watch a good movie I feel like I belong
> there more than I belong in my own life ...'

Hamish blushes deeply, and the other students laugh at what Bo has read out. Bo looks at Hamish, not mocking, but concerned. It's almost as if he regrets making the others laugh at him.

> BO
> Is your life really that bad?

Hamish grabs his essay back.

> HAMISH
> Better than yours.

He stands, quickly packing his things.

> KAZ
> Aren't we good enough for you?

HAMISH
I didn't say that.

He is about to leave when a tall, imposing man steps into shot, blocking his exit. The students are instantly wary and tense. He is MR CUSHING, the school bursar. The students do not like him, and he definitely does not like them.

MR CUSHING
Everything all right here?

The students look down at their things, avoiding his eyes. Cushing stares at Kaz, and she squirms, uncomfortable with his attention. He speaks, not taking his eyes off her.

MR CUSHING
There's been another robbery ...

STUDENT 1
From the lockers again?

MR CUSHING
Yes. Obviously there's a student here we can't trust.

Hamish looks from Kaz to Cushing. What's the bursar's problem? Is he trying to say she's the thief?

MR CUSHING
Kaz Murneau, could I have a quiet word with you?

> KAZ
> (sighs)
> Okay.

Kaz stands and leaves with Cushing. The students huddle, ignoring Hamish.

> STUDENT 2
> He's always picking on her.

> STUDENT 1
> You don't think he ...

Bo reacts angrily to their gossiping.

> BO
> Kaz hasn't done anything wrong!

The students apologise, but Bo is looking at Hamish. He seems to be trying to say something with his look, but Hamish just shrugs and leaves, going to his locker to check if everything is there. He opens the locker and finds a piece of paper inside. See Hamish's reaction as he reads the paper. He looks worried. See a close-up of the note on the paper:

> **Meet tonight at 10.00 p.m. at the top of the BUYGOOD car park. You have been chosen to fight evil. This is not a prank!**

End on a close-up of Hamish's face.

3

Scene three

It had to have been Bo who left the note, or maybe Kaz. They were playing some kind of prank on him. No doubt they were waiting somewhere in the car park with a video camera, ready to get some shots of the foolish Hamish being sucked in by a mysterious message. Secret notes about fighting evil and meetings in empty car parks were the stuff of overworked imaginations ... or movies.

Hamish lay back on his bed. If kids like Kaz and Bo took the time to get to know him, they'd see that he wasn't always so serious. It was hard to be his old self, there was too much to deal with. And to make it worse, whenever he was nervous he tensed up. His dad had once said to him, 'You know, Hamish, the real you is as funny as a good comedy on the TV, but the nervous you is like watching a documentary on the mating cycle of ants.'

Why couldn't he be like Kaz? Everyone liked her. She had heaps of friends, and she always seemed relaxed ... except when Cushing was around. Hamish remembered how the bursar had stared at Kaz. It was so creepy. There was something about that man that wasn't right. Everyone felt it. He was more than just creepy or bad-tempered. He seemed ... well ... evil.

Hamish sat up. Evil. Could it mean ...? Oh, come on! This was ridiculous. He was not going to walk to that stupid car park and meet some stupid person all because of a stupid note that said he had to fight evil. The note wasn't even real! He told himself this fact, even as he was putting on his jacket. The note was just a set-up to make him look silly. He reminded himself of this, even as he was sneaking down the hallway to the front door, the sounds of Aunt Jenny's snoring muffled in the background.

He reached the front door and paused, thinking everything through. If it was just a prank, then no doubt his classmates expected him *not* to turn up. They thought he was a stuck-up, unadventurous little twerp who would never dare sneak out at night on his own. A slow anger boiled in him. He'd show them who was stuck-up! He'd show them the *real* Hamish.

Imagining that he was some kind of hero in a movie, Hamish flung the door wide open, but it banged against the wall with a loud crash. He froze. The rhythmic snores from his auntie's bedroom wafted down the hall. He closed the door gently and set off.

Outside, the streets were nearly empty, and only the occasional car passed him. He'd never done anything like this before. Back home he wouldn't have even contemplated it, but there was something about living so far away from your family. You had to grow up a lot quicker. And that meant taking some risks. Sure, Aunt Jenny might find out. Or worse, his classmates might laugh at him. He promised himself that whatever happened that night, at the very least it would be a good idea for a video.

Cheered by this thought, Hamish walked quickly to his rendezvous. An empty car park, a mysterious person, and destiny lay ahead of him.

Just your usual Tuesday night, really.

4

Scene four

Inside the darkened car park, a car rolls in silently. It stops before a puddle, and is reflected in the water like a gothic monster. The headlights are flicked off, leaving the car hidden in the shadows. A door opens ...

The note-writer steps out.

The note has worked.

'Here he comes ...'

'... the next hero.'

Hamish didn't know whether to be surprised or alarmed by the fact that the car park door was unlocked. He pushed it open carefully, calling out, 'Hello?' There was no answer. Then he remembered that he was supposed to meet his mysterious note-writer on the top floor. Hamish trudged up the pitch-black stairway, feeling his way cautiously. It was slow going, hands out in front of him, heart racing, feet feeling for each step.

By the time he reached the top of the stairs, Hamish was exhausted. He opened the door to the top floor, and was disappointed to see it was completely empty. A few pathetic light bulbs struggled to illuminate the area. He'd expected to at least see Kaz or Bo, or hear some distant giggling, or even see a mysterious figure in the shadows ...

'Shut the door and step under the nearest light.'

Hamish looked to see that a mysterious figure was indeed standing in the shadows. He shivered a little, then took a tentative step forward. He could feel the light bulb above him.

'Good.' The voice sounded old, but not too old. One thing was for certain, it was not Kaz or Bo.

'Now I know I've truly flipped,' muttered Hamish.

'You haven't flipped,' said the voice. 'This is quite possibly the smartest thing you've ever done in your life.'

'Oh, sure,' said Hamish. He scanned the shadowy figure, but couldn't see any facial details. 'Okay, who are you and what do you want?'

'I don't want anything,' said the voice. 'And as for who I am ... you can call me "First Director" for now.'

Hamish snorted with laughter. 'First Director, eh?

You'd have to be a senior student at Capra with a name like that. And modest too.'

'You'll understand ... in time,' said First Director.

'Yes, very mysterious and all that,' said Hamish. 'I suppose you've got a hidden camera somewhere? And this will be a great piece of entertainment tomorrow ...'

'No!' First Director's booming voice echoed around the empty car park. 'That's the first rule. No-one must know. Never tell anyone. Never reveal who you are.'

'Oh, please,' groaned Hamish. 'Enough with the cloak and dagger. Where did you get these lines from? Some old black and white movie?'

'Shut up and listen!' snapped the voice. 'You have been chosen. You are one of the four. This is Capra High's secret ...'

'And what exactly have I been chosen for? Nerd of the week?' asked Hamish.

The voice did not answer. Instead, something flew out of the darkness, hitting Hamish on the shoulder.

'Hey!' he yelled.

'Pick it up.'

Hamish bent and picked up a plastic CD case. He opened it to see that it contained a Digital Video Disc. 'So?' he said. 'You've thrown me a DVD. What's on it? Your graduation film?'

First Director sighed loudly in the shadows, then said, 'That's no ordinary DVD, Hamish. It's a Vidz.'

'Vidz, schmidz,' said Hamish. 'What's on it?'

'Take it home,' commanded First Director. 'But you must watch it alone!'

'How about I don't watch it?'

'You believe, Hamish. That's why you're here. You believe, so you'll watch it. Remember your essay?'

'My essay?' shrieked Hamish. 'Is there anyone in the world who hasn't read my essay?'

'Watch the Vidz. If you panic, just yell "Cut". Meet me here tomorrow night, same time.'

'Oh sure,' sneered Hamish. 'Meet you again so you can add to your collection of "Dumb Hamish" videos ...'

He was cut short by the sound of a car door slamming. An engine burst into life, revving loudly, before a sleek black car with tinted windows sped out of the darkness and down the exit ramp. Hamish was blinded by the sudden glare of its lights.

'Don't suppose you could give me a lift?' he called, just for the fun of it. He pulled the DVD out of the plastic case and turned it over. There were no markings — no title or scrawled name of an owner. What had First Director called it? A Vidz?

'Doesn't matter what snazzy name it's got,' said Hamish. 'I bet it'll still be boring.'

5

Scene five

Okay, so he'd watch the stupid video. What harm could it do? He was in his room, his bedroom door was shut and Aunt Jenny was peacefully snoring over the hall.

Hamish booted up his computer, then inserted the DVD and waited. The viewing screen popped up, and he clicked it to full screen, thinking he might as well get the 'full' experience. He selected *play* with the mouse.

Nothing happened. The screen was black. 'Very entertaining so far,' he muttered. He was about to eject the DVD when a simple, white title appeared on the screen: 'First Director'. These words slowly dissolved into a new one: 'Vidz'.

'Ho hum,' sighed Hamish.

The screen was black again. Then a loud fanfare blasted from the computer's speakers. A tall youth appeared on the screen, standing in a battlefield. He looked eighteen or so, and had a thin scar across his cheek. His hair was wild and scraggly, and he held an enormous sword with both hands. He was breathing heavily, and looked near to exhausted. Obviously he was in the middle of some kind of fight.

Hamish leaned forward as the camera zoomed out to show a wide shot of the battle scene. There was something familiar about the youth's face. Enemies surrounded him, desperate men in dull armour with beaten metal helmets covering half their faces, backed up by fierce goblins in chain-mail shirts. They looked like terrifying opponents, armed with swords and spikes. This guy didn't stand a chance alone. A hard look of determination came over his face as he scanned his circle of foes, then he shouted, 'For my king!' Suddenly he swung his massive sword and fierce white light glowed across the screen. Dramatic music started playing. Then the picture froze and the title, *A Dangerous Secret*, appeared.

'Could be interesting,' said Hamish.

He wondered who this lone swordsman was, and why everyone wanted to kill him. He didn't mind a bit of a sword fight, and these sorts of movies always had plenty of them. 'Come on, Vidz,' he said. 'Surprise me.'

Nothing in the world could have prepared Hamish

for the surprise that was in store for him. A strange throbbing started pounding in his temples, and his vision grew blurry and dim.

'Whoa! What's going on?'

All he could see now was a fuzzy light coming from somewhere in the room, most probably the computer monitor. Hamish rubbed his eyes, but nothing worked. His vision only grew worse. The vague, flickering light seemed to be growing larger and larger, as if the computer was moving towards him.

Or I'm falling into it, thought Hamish.

The rest of his room was pitch black. There was only that blurry light, moving closer, closer, zooming in on him. A faraway sound rang in his ears. It was a voice ... Falling? Calling? Crying out? The voice was emitting one long, loud call. 'Aaaaaaaaaaa ...' It began to hurt Hamish's ears. 'Aaaaaaaa ...' When would it end? Finally the noise formed into words. 'Aaaaaand action!' Without warning, the light hurtled towards him at great speed, and Hamish let out a cry. Something hit him in the face, sending him sprawling backwards onto the dusty, hard ground.

Onto the ground?

Scene six

Hamish sat bolt upright and looked around. He was in the middle of a dirt road. All around him were wide open fields with grazing cows and sheep. Everything looked peaceful and calm in the bright afternoon sunlight.

'Now *this* is what I call a realistic movie experience,' said Hamish.

A muffled drumming noise sounded, growing louder and louder by the second. The ground began to vibrate, and small rocks started bouncing about. Was it an earthquake? Hamish turned round in time to see a black carriage pulled by a team of horses thundering towards him. With a short scream he leapt for the side of the road as the carriage roared past, its wheel clipping him on the heel.

'Get off the road, you lout!' bellowed a harsh voice.

Lout? thought Hamish. *Who's he calling a lout?* This movie was getting too real. He sat up and shook his fist at the departing carriage.

'Thanks for nothing!' shouted Hamish.

Who the heck said that? Hamish looked around. That voice ... it certainly wasn't his. The sound that had emerged from his mouth was a deep, sharp voice. Hamish took a breath and tried saying something else.

'Hello?' There it was again — a man's voice! How could he have a man's voice? Then again, how had he managed to land in the middle of the countryside on a sunny day?

This isn't really happening, thought Hamish. He knew it was just a dream, or a nightmare, or he was unconscious, or something. Still, all around him were birds singing and flies buzzing. He got up from the side of the road, only to discover that he'd landed in a cow pat when he'd done his spectacular dive. It smelled very real.

'Oh ... yuck!' he yelled, scraping the green-brown muck from his tunic.

His tunic!

Hamish examined his clothing. He was wearing tights, and a plain, smock-like tunic with a huge leather belt around it. He had a leather pouch around his neck, and wore a gold ring with a dark stone embedded in it.

Obviously fashion isn't important in this movie, he thought.

That's when it hit him. He was dreaming that he'd

landed inside the Vidz movie ... Either that, or he really *was* in the Vidz.

'Whatever,' shrugged Hamish. 'I might as well enjoy myself.'

As he had no idea what to do next, he decided to head in the direction of the afternoon sun. With any luck he might accidentally wander back to his bedroom. After a few minutes of strolling down the dusty road, keeping an ear out for any more thundering carriages and grumpy drivers, he came to some form of civilisation. It wasn't a city, or even a village, but a quaint little building made of rough, vertical planks, with a low, thatched roof. A wooden sign hung outside the door: 'The Royal Dagger'.

Common sense told him to steer clear of a place called the Royal Dagger. It could only spell trouble. No doubt it was an inn, or a tavern, or something like that. It'd be full of men drinking beer, loud conversation, awful smells. Hamish went to walk on past the Royal Dagger, but his feet started dragging in the dirt. He had a powerful urge to go back and taste a long, cold pitcher of ale, tangy and refreshing and ...

Wait a minute! thought Hamish. *I've never drunk ale in my life*! How could he know what it tasted like, let alone want to have one? There was only one way to find out. He swung around and headed for the little building, stooping under the roofline to get to the door.

A polished shield was standing against the outside wall, and Hamish could see a tall stranger in its reflection. He stepped aside to allow the stranger through ... but nobody came. He turned and started to say, 'After you', but the words died on his lips.

Who goes there?

'After you ...'

There was nobody there. Hamish turned back to the shield. *He* was that tall stranger. And a young man! His heart started thumping loudly, and he felt as if he might faint. Pushing the wooden door aside, he stepped into the dim interior of the tavern and sat heavily on a short wooden stool. He tried to calm himself, but all he could think about was the image of that youth in the shield. How could he look like that? And so good-looking, too?

A squat, greasy landlord wearing a leather apron

approached him and spoke in a strange accent. 'By the king's good grace, what brings you to this house, Hamish?'

Hamish jumped with shock. He knew his name! How could he? Then he realised that he was a character in the Vidz movie, and the tall, scraggly-haired young man must be called Hamish too.

The landlord was rubbing his hands together nervously, as if he was waiting for Hamish to say something. What had he said to him? What brings you here?

'Why, I come for my thirst,' Hamish replied.

The landlord shook his head, and muttered, 'You are a brave man, Sir Champion.'

I'm a champion? thought Hamish. *Cool. But champion what? Cherry-spitter? Chicken-swinger?* Then he remembered the titles sequence, and the lone figure with the huge sword. There was something familiar about that guy. Hamish ran outside to look at his reflection in the shield again. It wasn't perfectly clear, but there was little doubting it. *He* was that lone swordsman. Hamish examined his face, tracing the thin scar across his cheek. It made him look handsome. Then he realised that the face he was looking at was his own, only slightly older. This was himself in a few years time as a young man. He liked what he saw.

Hamish returned to the tavern, deep in thought. The landlord was shaking his head, with a sad look on his face.

'They said that you had much changed,' he muttered. 'They said your mind was wandering. Had I not seen it with my own eyes ... You were once so bold and brave.'

'No braver than the next man,' whispered Hamish. *Where did that line come from?*

The landlord grunted. 'Mm ... perhaps that's a matter between you and the king. What can I get you for your thirst?'

For my thirst? He might as well try that ale he'd been dreaming about outside. But how should he ask? He had to sound like the character in the movie. Hamish coughed, then boomed in a loud voice, 'Ale for my health, and no questions asked!' *Hey, not bad.*

The landlord laughed. 'You always say that, Hamish. You always say, "And no questions asked." One day I'll give you a shock and ask a question.'

Not as much of a shock as I'm feeling now, thought Hamish.

Somehow he'd managed to say the exact words that the Vidz-Hamish always used. Perhaps he was able to be the character of Hamish without trying. Which was weird, but at least it meant he didn't have to worry too much about raising suspicion.

The landlord plonked a clay pitcher of dark beer in front of Hamish and said, 'You have coins?'

Hamish felt about in the leather pouch that hung from his neck. There was only a rusty old metal disc in there, and something lumpy that had worked its way into the stitching. He tried to extract it to see if it was money, but his fingers were too large. As there were no coins, he offered the metal disc. The landlord looked at it disdainfully.

'Okay. Put my ale down on the king's bill,' said Hamish with a shrug.

The landlord bent double with laughter, banging his fist on the rough wooden plank that acted as a counter.

It wasn't that funny, thought Hamish. The man was in danger of falling apart from mirth.

'On the king's bill,' shrieked the landlord. 'You jest and jape. Have this ale for free, because once you were the people's champion. The young Sir Hamish. Oh, how you were loved ...'

'I was?'

'Aye, I know ... it must seem an age ago, yet it was only last year.' The landlord leaned forward slightly and spoke in a low voice. 'The people still need a champion, Sir Hamish. There was a time when you rode tall on your stallion, ridding our land of evil horrors. Some said you had magic to help you ...'

Hamish closed his eyes, seeing himself on a magnificent horse, wielding his sword, killing goblins and demons and all sorts of nasties. He could almost hear the people cheering. He could almost see his enemies falling about him. 'How good was I?' he whispered.

'None could beat you,' said the landlord.

'And my sword?'

'Your blade was mighty. Hard, and sharp ... and cruel to the king's enemies. Well did it deserve the name "Justice".'

Hamish remembered the mighty sword that the lone swordsman held. Oh, how he'd love to get his hands on it again ... *Again? I've never touched the stupid thing!*

'You were always your own man,' continued the landlord. 'Proud ... noble ... took no counsel. It was your undoing in the end.'

Proud, thought Hamish. *Noble*. He liked the sound of his character, the people's champion.

'The people once cheered me!' he shouted, standing up. 'And they shall cheer me again!' He expected to hear stirring music, or crowds cheering, but there was nothing, except for the landlord's burp.

He sat down with a plonk on the stool. Sir Hamish must have fallen on hard times lately. Grabbing the clay pitcher, he drank deeply. The ale tasted surprisingly good, like honey and ginger beer and lemonade all rolled into one. He slammed the pitcher onto the bench and shouted, 'Another, my good man.'

The landlord laughed heartily. 'You are funny.'

Sure, I'm funny, thought Hamish as the landlord filled another pitcher. Which was more than he could say for this movie. So far it was about as funny as a leaking drain. Surely something would happen soon? The landlord leant closer to Hamish, his sour breath wafting over him in putrid waves. 'I like you, Sir Hamish,' he whispered. 'I always have.'

'Great,' said Hamish. 'You couldn't possibly like me over there, could you? Where I can't smell you?'

'You have many enemies,' continued the landlord in a putrid whisper. 'And none greater than your king. I wouldn't like to see you lose your head ...'

'Maybe that'd be a blessing,' said Hamish. 'At least my *nose* would go with it ...'

'Now that you have been set free to walk amongst the people again, watch what you say and do ... these are still dangerous times.'

'You breathe words of caution, good landlord,' said Hamish. 'Next time, write me a letter.'

The landlord grinned, his green, stumpy teeth so close

that Hamish could almost hear the fleas playing in their gaps. Any more of this secret conversation and he'd faint! The sound of a stool scraping beside him saved Hamish from further pong. The landlord shot a mean look sideways, then stood back with a glare at the new customer. Hamish turned to see an old, withered man sitting on the stool. There was an even worse stench coming from the man's filthy rags. His face was pocked and scarred, and his hair looked as though it had been washed in seaweed.

'So, you are here too,' snapped the landlord. 'You are less welcome than Sir Champion here.' Then he slunk off to pour a drink for the new arrival, who swivelled on his stool to face Hamish.

'Hamish,' grunted the horrible old man.

'Old John,' grunted Hamish in reply. *I know his name ... amazing.*

The landlord delivered a drink to Old John, who barely nodded in response. He seemed lost in his thoughts, as if he was debating something in his head. After a moment he leaned over towards Hamish, and the smell was like a fist to the stomach. It was all Hamish could do to keep himself from falling off the bar stool. *Thank goodness you don't get smell in real movies*, he thought.

'Did you think over our ... discussion?' asked Old John in a loud whisper.

Hamish racked his brain for a clue as to what Old John meant, but he came up blank. Clearly, being Hamish in the Vidz didn't allow him to know everything.

'Um ...' said Hamish. 'Perhaps I have thought it over. What exactly was it again?'

'You fool!' yelled Old John, grabbing Hamish by his shirt-front. 'Do you think I jest for your amusement?'

'No ... I think you hurt for my pain!'

'Hurt? I? Hurting you?'

'Well, actually, yes. You are hurting me,' said Hamish.

Old John laughed. 'The once great champion is feeling hurt. Our enemies quaked in their boots at the very sight of the young champion, Sir Hamish. Now they wouldn't even take the time to piddle on you.'

'Now, come on,' said Hamish. 'That's a bit harsh ... I'm sure they'd like to piddle on me.'

'I thought you could help. I thought you were a hero, but you are nothing but a stupid boy. A bag of wind. I spit on you ...'

'Please don't.'

'My life is in danger,' yelled Old John. 'Can't you see that?'

'I want to see it,' said Hamish through gritted teeth.

What was this guy's problem? Couldn't he just enjoy a quiet drink in the tavern without having to have a psychotic fit? Old John gripped Hamish's shirt tighter, twisting the fabric round in his fingers.

'Do you not remember?' shouted Old John. 'How I heard the evil lord plotting against our king? Do you not remember anything?'

'Just show me the script or something,' said Hamish. 'I've forgotten the back-story, that's all ...'

'Fool!' shouted Old John, exploding with anger. He pushed Hamish off his stool. 'The king should have executed you when he had the chance! You are a lonely piece of maggot dung!'

'Who are you calling lonely?' protested Hamish. 'I'm the people's champion ...'

'Your precious people sat on their fat backsides when you were rotting in that prison. Do you think they weep for you? Their bold champion is useless now. He has lost all his mighty powers. Evil grows in this land, and you do nothing. We'd be better off if you were dead, at least then we'd have the memory!' Old John stormed angrily out of the tavern.

Hamish sat for a moment, his head spinning, his heart racing. *Of course the people care about me*, he thought. Then he shook his head. It was only a movie, and he was only a character. But Old John's words had hurt. Hamish stood shakily. He wasn't lonely, and he hadn't lost his powers. People *did* still love him. He'd show that old beggar that there was still life left in the young Sir Hamish. He marched out of the tavern into the fading afternoon light.

A few cottages stood in a loose arrangement around an old well. It was there that Old John stood, staring gloomily down the shaft of the well. *He's not going to jump, is he?* thought Hamish. He rushed over to John, calling, 'Wait! I'm sorry. It's my memory ... it's not what it used to be.'

'You have gone soft in the head,' snapped Old John. 'How could you forget what I told you? Our king is in danger ...'

'It's coming back to me,' lied Hamish. 'Keep going.'

'Thank the good lord you are only fifty-fifth in line for the monarchy. Any closer and we'd be ruined.'

'Fifty-fifth?'

'Don't tell me you've even forgotten that you're the king's fourth cousin?'

'How could I forget that?' said Hamish, rather pleased with the way he was acting out his part. 'Listen, Old John. The king must know our news. Tell me the details again ...'

'Are you sure you will remember?' asked Old John.

'Absolutely sure.'

'The plot to assassinate King Ronald ... it is set for the feast. That's only two days away! We will be doomed if King Ronald dies. The evil Dudley will take over the land. Surely you still remember what Dudley has done to our people? Anyone who opposes him is brutally crushed. He has secret bands of soldiers who burn and cause terror at his call. He has powers that none dare whisper about. Dudley is your mortal enemy!'

Hamish tried to remember what this Dudley looked like, but his mind was a blank. He sounded like all the evil rulers who still had power in the real world.

'You must go to the castle yourself and warn the king,' pleaded Old John. He clutched at his throat suddenly, a strange, gurgling sound coming from his lips.

'What's wrong?' asked Hamish.

'I ... the feast day ...' Old John turned a deathly pale colour.

'Old John? Old John? Are you all right?'

'... the plot ... there's one more thing ... Who will you trust ... ?'

'What? Who will I trust?'

The old man jerked his head back as though he'd been punched, then fell to the ground. Dead.

Heavy footsteps approached the well. Hamish heard voices shouting. A mob of angry villagers surrounded him, looks of accusation on their faces. 'What have you done to Old John?' they cried, pointing to his body on the ground.

'I ...' stammered Hamish, looking around at the angry, strange faces.

'They were arguing in the tavern,' cried the landlord.

'Now he's dead!' shouted someone in the mob.

'You killed him!' shouted another.

'No!'

'Murderer! Murderer!'

'I was your champion.'

'Let's hang him high!'

'Cut!' yelled Hamish at the top of his voice. 'Cut! Cut! Cut!'

His vision blurred and the strangers around him seemed to shimmer and shake, then all went black.

7

Scene seven

From the moment he reappeared in his bedroom that night, still shouting, 'Cut! Cut!', Hamish refused to believe the Vidz had been real. He made up a thousand excuses for what had happened. The whole experience had simply been a product of his imagination, that was all. But when he tried to sleep that night, nightmares about Old John and lynch mobs kept him tossing about in his bed.

He woke the next morning feeling lousy, and went to school a physical wreck. Then, to make matters worse, he'd somehow left his essay at home when he repacked his bag that morning. A late essay meant zero. He had until the end of lunch to hand it in, otherwise he was history. He ran home to Aunt Jenny's at lunchtime, grabbed the essay, then made it back to the school panting heavily. Bo was sitting on the lawn outside the school when Hamish returned, and he asked, 'What's the hurry?', but Hamish just ignored him.

When he tried to get into the school he found that all the doors were locked. This was part of Cushing's new security regime. An older boy was guarding the doorway. He was probably a senior student, although he wasn't in uniform.

'Please,' begged Hamish, holding out his essay for the senior student to see. 'I've *got* to hand this in.'

The older student looked about nervously, as if he was afraid of his own shadow. He hardly seemed the 'guard' type, more a wimpy loner who'd been roped into the job by Cushing because no-one else would do it.

'I'm sorry,' he said in a soft voice. 'Mr Cushing's orders ...'

'But I have to ...'

'Sorry.'

Hamish glared at him, then walked away, wandering around the building until he found a window open in the girls' toilet. He stood on a rubbish bin and pushed himself in, landing with a crash onto the floor. Ignoring the pain in his shoulder, Hamish walked calmly out into the corridor and made his way towards the office. So much for the guard and the locked doors. Hamish grinned to himself. He liked taking action. Yesterday he wouldn't have dreamed of breaking in. Could watching the Vidz do that? Hamish shrugged as he headed for the teachers' pigeonholes.

His footsteps echoed loudly around the empty corridors, mingling with another sound. It was coming from the lockers area. Was it the thief? Hamish took up a position behind a pillar to check out what was happening, peering out cautiously. That was no student at the lockers, it was Cushing. What was he doing? Looking for stolen stuff? Hamish snuck out a little further and realised that Cushing was at Kaz's locker.

This guy must really hate her, thought Hamish.

He'd just have to sit it out, that was all. Cushing wouldn't take forever. He slid down onto the ground behind the pillar and twiddled his thumbs. After a brief wait, a voice spoke from above him.

'Mr Wajda. What are you doing in here?'

Hamish leapt up, his tongue tripping over a hundred excuses for why he'd broken into the school at lunchtime. This was bad. VERY bad. He could be thrown out for this, accused of being the thief.

'I was … I mean … I want to … I was going to … my essay. Sir. Hand it in, that is …'

He held up the troublesome essay, and Cushing snatched it from him, reading over the words, a sick smile on his face. Hamish wanted to protest. After all, Cushing was only the bursar, and not a teacher. He was supposed to look after property and materials, and leave essays to the staff.

'So … you'd rather live in a movie, eh?' said Cushing.

Hamish groaned. This was becoming a standing joke now.

'It's just an essay, sir ...'

'Oh, I disagree, Mr Wajda. You see, I know exactly what you are trying to say here.'

'Oh,' said Hamish, wondering what was going to come next. Would the bursar march him off to the Principal's office? Would he call the police? Or had he believed him about the late essay?

'Time to run along now, Mr Wajda,' said the bursar. 'I'll make sure your essay arrives on time.'

Hamish wanted to cry with relief, but a horrid smile on the bursar's face stalled the celebration for the moment.

'I've got my eye on you, young man,' said Mr Cushing. 'You could go far.'

Hamish nodded his head, trying to hide his disgust at the smarmy, arrogant bursar. He left in double time and made it back to the girls' toilet, leaning against the wall, panting. That bursar was maximum creepy. He was about to climb back out the window when he stopped. A weird feeling in the pit of Hamish's stomach bothered him ... something was wrong. What was Cushing *really* doing at the lockers? Any sensible student would leave straight away and forget about the bursar. Hamish headed back for the lockers.

The area was deserted. He went to Kaz's locker. It looked perfectly normal. No sign of anyone breaking into it. But then again, Cushing would have a key. Hamish paced up and down in front of the locker, cursing himself for ever coming back.

'I should have just left it alone,' he muttered. What did he think he was? Some kind of hero? He pulled out his own key and twisted it around in Kaz's lock. 'One minute,' he told himself. 'Then I go.' The bell would be ringing soon, and everyone would be streaming back into the building. Hamish twisted harder, cursing, until ... snap! The key broke inside Kaz's lock.

'This couldn't get any worse,' moaned Hamish as he extracted his broken key from the lock. That's when he heard the sound of the school bell ringing. He screamed with frustration, banging the locker door with his fist, cursing it for not opening. Suddenly the door sprang open and Hamish almost laughed with relief.

He had to hurry, the corridor would be filled with people any second. Looking inside the locker, he found one of the school's expensive professional digicams. Students in Hamish's year weren't allowed to book out the digicams without a teacher supervising. They were worth many thousands of dollars. Cushing had probably planted it there to get Kaz expelled. Then again, what if Kaz had put the camera there? She said yesterday that she was in debt.

Hamish removed the camera. Whatever happened, it had to go back to its rightful place. He was wondering where to put it when the corridor burst into life, a pack of noisy students filling the empty spaces. He quickly grabbed a jumper that was lying on top of the lockers and wrapped the camera in it. Then he pushed Kaz's locker shut, hearing at that moment the sound he'd been dreading.

'What are you doing?'

It was Kaz. She ran to him, her face red with fury.

'Nothing ... I ... I noticed that the door was open,' lied Hamish. 'So I closed it.'

Kaz flung her locker open and quickly checked its contents, then shook her head. 'Nothing's missing,' she muttered, a strange look on her face. She stood up and regarded Hamish suspiciously. 'How come you were in the building so quickly?'

Hamish blushed a deep red, and looked about at the gathering crowd. Any second now they'd notice the camera hidden in his hands. 'I'm not a thief,' he yelled.

'No-one's called you a thief ...'

'No? Well, you're implying it.' It was time to go. He turned quickly and marched away. Thankfully no-one followed him.

He looked at the camera in his hands. What should he do with it? Take it to the Principal? It was definite proof that either Cushing had tried to frame Kaz, or Kaz was the thief. So which story should he tell? It was all too confusing. Hamish paused outside the Principal's office. You had to be very brave, or very stupid, to make accusations against Cushing. He took a deep breath, then walked past the Principal's door to the camera store, returning the camera with a feeble story about finding it in one of the studios.

By the time Hamish walked home at the end of the day he was in a miserable mood. Then he opened the front door and was greeted by a delicious cooking smell. It was such a normal, homely scene — Aunt Jenny home early, standing at the stove whistling a happy tune — that Hamish felt his whole body release the tension from the day.

'I hope you're hungry, Hame,' she called. 'Because I've gone berserk here!'

Hamish looked around the kitchen. Every available surface was covered in a messy pot or pan. And guess who had the job of doing the dishes? He sighed. At least the food smelled good.

They ate early, and Hamish had two helpings of his aunt's chicken and vegetable curry, which was just as well because he needed all the strength he could muster to deal with the aftermath. Aunt Jenny grabbed herself a glass of wine as Hamish slaved over the wreckage of the kitchen.

'So,' she said in her cheerful voice. 'Make any movies today?'

The image of the Vidz flashed into Hamish's mind, and he quickly thought of something else. Capra, his classes, the shooting they'd already done.

'We shoot little video exercises,' he said. 'To learn how to do it properly. Most of us taught ourselves before we came, but the teachers want us to learn the basics. Some of the other kids are bored by that, but I don't mind. After all, I came to Capra to learn ...'

'Good for you, Hame,' said his auntie. 'I'm looking forward to watching you receive your first award ...'

'You'll have to wait for a while,' laughed Hamish. 'There's a few things I have to do first ... like these dishes!'

Aunt Jenny smiled, but she didn't offer to help. 'I hope you don't mind if I don't keep you company,' she said. 'My favourite TV show is on. You won't be lonely, will you?'

'Not at all,' said Hamish, up to his elbows in mucky dishwater. This was nothing compared to how lonely he was at school. Hamish the weirdo. Hamish the stuck-up know-it-all! Hamish the suspected thief. Somehow it all seemed to be connected to the Vidz. The mysterious First Director had told him he'd been 'chosen'. Chosen for what? To lead a miserable life?

I'll trash that Vidz straight after the dishes, thought Hamish as he scrubbed the large rice pot. And First Director, or whatever, can sit in the car park alone tonight.

He decided to focus on happy thoughts as he washed the dishes — his mum and dad, his old dog — but the images from the Vidz kept crashing through. Old John lying on the ground, strangers shouting at him, the landlord's breathy whispers, the dangerous secret that Old John had told him: the king was about to be murdered by an assassin. If he died, then the land would fall under the evil rule of Lord Dudley. There was so little time left ... everything hinged on the feast, only two days away!

Whoa! Wait on! thought Hamish, shaking his head. *What am I doing? It's just a movie! It's not real!*

He stormed to his room after the dishes and slammed the door behind him, picking up the Vidz and staring at it.

'You're going into the bin,' said Hamish grimly. Then he noticed some small, black writing on the DVD. It hadn't been there last night. Hamish held the DVD up and read the tiny words printed in flowing script: 'This Vidz belongs to First Director, Hamish Wajda.'

'What the heck is that?' shouted Hamish, throwing

the Vidz onto the bed. It landed on the teddy's nose, knocking it sideways.

'Sorry, Hitchcock,' said Hamish, flinging the Vidz off the bed. He picked the teddy up, and noticed that one of his little glass eyes was missing. Hamish searched under the bed, thinking the eye must have been knocked out when he flung the Vidz, but he didn't find it. Climbing back onto the bed, he lay with his head on Hitchcock's soft belly. Everything was getting crazy. *He* wasn't First Director, the mysterious voice in the car park was First Director. Who'd gone and written all over the Vidz? And when did they do it?

There was only one way to find out. He switched his little portable TV on loud, then padded out of his bedroom and grabbed his coat, shutting the front door quietly behind him. Hopefully Aunt Jenny would think he was watching a movie in his room.

He was going to have a few words with this mysterious First Director, that was all. There was no way he was entering that Vidz again to be hanged. The people could starve or be murdered for all he cared. He was Hamish Wajda, a student who happened to like movies. Nothing more.

8

Scene eight

Hamish nearly ran up the pitch-black stairway of the car park, bursting through the door onto the fifth floor. The voice of First Director greeted him the moment he emerged into the light.

'You watched the video.'

'How can you be so sure?' asked Hamish.

'It has your name on it.'

'Yes it does. How did you know?'

'I know because you are First Director now.'

'Oh yeah? So what do I call you, then?' asked Hamish.

A young man stepped out into the light. 'You can call me Michael,' he said. It was the wimpy senior student who Cushing had given the job of guarding the door to.

'You?' said Hamish. 'You were First Director?'

'Surprised?' said Michael. 'You should be. I've worked hard at making people think I'm a quiet, nerdy type. You have to keep your Vidz life a total secret. And that might mean hiding your true self.'

He pulled a package out of his backpack and tossed it to Hamish.

'What's this?' said Hamish. He opened the package and found three more DVDs inside. 'More Vidz?' he asked.

'For the other three directors,' said Michael.

'Aw, come on,' groaned Hamish. 'What other directors? Who are they? Can't they come and get them from you?'

'No,' he answered. 'That's your responsibility now. You are First Director. The leader of the team. You have a big job ahead of you, and it won't be easy ... but it will be amazing.'

Hamish wasn't sure, but he thought he could detect a slightly relieved and happy note in Michael's voice. 'So, what about your team?' he said. 'Where are they?'

'They've all graduated,' said Michael. 'I have too, but I took on a job at the school so I could pass on the Vidz.'

'You're not a student?'

'I was,' said Michael. 'That's how Vidz work. Only Capra students can be Vidz directors. There's some kind of magic in the place ...'

'Listen,' said Hamish. 'That's very mysterious and all that, but I'm not sure if I want this job. Okay? So far I've had a very weird experience in a movie about a champion and a mysterious magic that no-one will talk about ... and what else? Oh yeah, a mob tried to lynch me! It's not that much fun!'

Michael smiled at him. 'Hamish,' he said. 'That's only the beginning of the Vidz. You haven't finished it yet.'

'Finished it?' shrieked Hamish. 'There's no way I'm finishing it. I don't care who's chosen me ...'

'You chose yourself.'

'Aw, come on!' shouted Hamish. 'That is just nuts.' He shook his head in frustration. Why couldn't he just get a straight answer to a straight question? How the heck did he choose himself?

'Don't you get it, Hamish?' whispered Michael. 'You believe. It's the only weapon against the enemy.'

Hamish sat down on the concrete floor. It was dirty and greasy, but right at that moment he didn't care. His head was spinning with a million questions and thoughts. Suddenly there was an 'enemy' to worry about. Something told him that if he asked who the enemy was, he'd get another one of those roundabout, confusing answers. But he gave it a try anyway.

'Okay,' said Hamish. 'I'm chosen because I believe ... and believing will beat the enemy. Any chance you could tell me who the enemy is in ten words or less?'

Michael laughed, and Hamish's hopes sank. Obviously a short answer was out of the question.

'The enemy,' he said. 'You see the enemy every day. The enemy is the murderer in the dark, the evil alien, the gangland boss, the corrupt politician, the ruthless opponent, the vicious ruler, the master of evil. It is the universal bad guy. He is a she, and she is a he. He is the last person you suspected, or the person you suspected all along.'

Great, thought Hamish. *Another riddle*. He wondered what Michael had meant by a universal bad guy. All those descriptions — gangland boss, evil alien, master of evil — they sounded like characters in movies. Then the truth hit him. They *were* characters in movies. What was going on here?

'Wait on a minute,' said Hamish. 'I don't know if you've seen your psychiatrist lately, but bad guys in movies are just in movies. They're NOT REAL!'

'Aren't they?' said Michael. 'What about last night, Hamish? Was that just a movie? Or did it feel real?'

Hamish shuddered. Last night had felt very real, especially when the mob were baying for his blood.

'You have to go back to the Vidz, Hamish. You have to complete it and defeat the evil ... defeat the bad guy.'

'Why do I have to?' asked Hamish. 'So what if the bad guy wins in this dumb movie? Who cares?'

Michael sighed loudly. 'That's where you're wrong. It's not a movie, it's a Vidz. Everything that happens in that Vidz has a mirror in real life. You let evil win in the Vidz, and evil will win in life.'

'Oh great,' said Hamish. 'Now I'm the only sucker who can beat evil.' It didn't make sense. 'I'm just an ordinary student at Capra Video School. Couldn't some superhero or something take care of this? I'm just a kid.'

'Which is why you are strong. I was a kid once, but I'm too old now. You're fresh, Hamish. You believe. That is your weapon, because the enemy also believes. He or she believes in evil, and knows if evil wins in the Vidz, then evil wins in your back yard. The Vidz team hasn't operated since graduation last year, and evil has had a chance to grow. Capra High is in danger. You're First Director of the Vidz now, you have to go back and defeat Dudley ... That's how you'll save Capra ...'

'Stop!' said Hamish, holding up his hand. All this stuff about Dudley and Capra in danger, and evil and Vidz ... His head was spinning. 'If I go back,' he continued slowly, 'I'll be killed. Lynched. There's a mob of very smelly villagers who'd like to put a rope round my neck.'

Michael stifled a laugh, then spoke in measured tones. 'Who says they'll lynch you in the Vidz? You can run, can't you? You'll learn ... you'll see how it all fits in. So will the other directors ...'

'There you go again,' said Hamish. 'Who are these other directors? Do they know that they're directors? Or can I give these Vidz to anyone I choose?'

'You could give a Vidz to anyone you choose, but it wouldn't mean anything to them. They'd just return it and say it didn't work. That's the way it is with Vidz. You will find the other directors, or they'll find you. Remember, four Vidz, four directors. You'll become a team ... in time.'

'Gee, I'm soooooo lucky,' said Hamish.

Michael nodded his head, ignoring Hamish's sarcasm. 'Yes,' he said. 'You are. My time as a director is over now, and I wish you all the luck. One day you'll stand here and say these same words to a complete stranger. And you'll feel the same way I do. But in the meantime, enjoy the most incredible ride of your life.'

Michael turned to go to his car, and Hamish said, 'Is that it?' Michael nodded, hopped in, and drove away.

'Thanks for the lift!' shouted Hamish.

He looked at the DVDs in his hands. Now he had four Vidz, but only one belonged to him. He clutched them to his chest and walked home. What a choice he had. Ignore the Vidz and let evil grow in the world. And worse. What had Michael said? Capra was in danger? Just like the kingdom was in danger. So there was an evil Lord Dudley in the Vidz, and someone evil at Capra.

A tangy mixture of fear and anticipation filled Hamish's mouth. He had a chance to save his school, and to save a kingdom where he was the people's champion. He could be a glorious hero, or wind up dead in a ditch.

One thing was for certain: life would never be the same again.

9

Scene nine

As soon as he returns, the ugly mob take up the chase.

The champion sees an escape.

A cave of sheets shall be his refuge.

It was a perfect hiding spot. The washerwoman, who had been bending over her basket throughout Hamish's brilliant escape, looked up to see a crowd of shouting villagers leaping her wall and running towards her. They swarmed into her yard like angry ants, shouting, 'Where is he?'

'Where is who?' asked the washerwoman.

Hamish listened from inside his wet-sheet cave as the crowd interrogated the washerwoman, demanding to know where 'Hamish the murderer!' was. What should he do now? Run? Surely they'll come to realise that he hid in here? Where else could he have gone? His brilliant plan was starting to look flimsy now.

The washerwoman sounded confused by the villagers' questions, asking them to repeat themselves over and over. She really wasn't very bright. 'I may have seen a man run that way into the woods,' she said. 'But it could have been a deer buck ...'

Surely the villagers weren't going to be convinced by that? They'd peer into his sheet cave any second now. Hamish crouched, ready to burst free, but to his amazement the villagers started saying, 'I saw a man go that way as well', and 'It must be Hamish'. Somehow the washerwoman had managed to fool them. 'After him!' came the shout, and the angry mob moved on.

How easy was that? thought Hamish. Now all he had to do was sit back and wait for the washerwoman to go inside. Then he would be free to ... to do what? Look for the 'bad guy'? Hamish sighed. It would help if he knew where to find the bad guy in this movie. What was his name again? Dudley? So all he had to do was go to the castle, warn the king about the assassination, find this Dudley character and save the day. Should be a snap.

Somebody point me to the castle, thought Hamish.

But nobody pointed him anywhere. Instead a face poked its way between two wet sheets and grinned at him.

'It's been a long time, Hamish my love,' whispered the washerwoman. 'You'd better tell me what mischief you've been having.'

Hamish stood sheepishly and followed the woman to her cottage. *Mischief? Oh, nothing much. I killed an old man simply by looking at him, or so it seems. And now your neighbours want to test how strong my neck is with a rope ...*

He entered the cottage, where the washerwoman was pouring him a pitcher of water. Hamish sat and took the drink greedily, his mouth suddenly dry. He emptied the pitcher before the woman had a chance to put the jug back on the sideboard.

'You have a thirst, my love,' she said, a look of worry on her face.

Hamish wiped his mouth with the back of his hand and said, 'Another.'

The washerwoman refilled the pitcher, then cut some hard cheese with a knife and placed it before him.

'Some cheese, my love?' she said.

Now he felt hungry, and took a piece of cheese, nearly cracking his teeth as he bit it. This was *hard* cheese. Hamish looked at this strange woman. She obviously knew young Hamish the champion very well, judging by all the 'my loves' she threw into the conversation.

'How did you do that?' he asked after finishing off half the cheese.

'Do what?' she said, carving up a large black loaf of bread.

'You fooled those people into thinking I went into the woods.'

'The mob was desperate to find you,' said the woman. 'They would have followed their own shadow ... All I can think is that they saw something and thought it was you.'

She smiled at him, but even behind her warm and pleasant nature, Hamish could see there was more to her story. She seemed to shimmer in the right light, as if there was a powerful glow to her that she kept hidden. She was quite beautiful, now that he looked at her, with long, raven-coloured hair that hung nearly to her waist. Her eyes were coal-black, and deep with sadness. And her skin was so pale that Hamish thought he could see her veins underneath, but maybe that was another trick of the light.

She sat beside him and took hold of his rough hand, stroking it gently. Her skin felt as soft as velvet, and Hamish nearly cried out with the shock of it. He studied her face, willing himself to remember who she was. *I know her, but how*? Snatches of good memories came to him, happy times, peaceful times, all associated with her. If only he knew her name. He liked sitting with her, liked holding her hand, liked the way she smiled at him. Could the Vidz do that? Could it make him 'know' a character from a movie?

He racked his brain. What was her name? Jenny?

Kate? Mary? Frances? Suddenly a strange-sounding name came to him. *It's worth a try*, thought Hamish.

'This is fine cheese, Beatrice,' said Hamish, and she smiled.

Got it!

'So, why does half the village chase you?' she asked with a mischievous smile.

Hamish debated whether or not he should tell her, but somehow he thought she probably knew already. Old John had asked him a strange question. 'Who will you trust?' He was alone in this Vidz, and yet he felt so much warmth from Beatrice. He decided to tell her about the plot. At the very least she could tell him where the castle was. When he had finished the story about the assassination, Beatrice looked deeply into his eyes, as if she were trying to read his thoughts.

'So,' she said after a while of this. 'What will you do now that Old John has mysteriously died for telling you his secret?'

Hamish sighed, then spoke in a gloomy voice. 'I don't know. But whatever I do, it has to be before the feast. Maybe I should tell the police ... '

'Police? What are they?'

Right. No police in this Vidz. He had to be very careful otherwise he'd give himself away. Who would he tell? The army? The king? Why not? After all, Sir Hamish was King Ronald's fourth cousin.

'I'll go straight to the king and warn him,' said Hamish.

'You'll what?' shrieked Beatrice, leaping into the air, causing the clay pitchers and plates to jump and rattle.

'Oh, Hamish, this is not time for jokes.'

'But the king is in trouble ... why wouldn't I tell him?'

She stared at Hamish with an incredulous look on her face and asked, 'Are you serious?'

'It's the only way. I'm sure that's why Old John told me his secret ...' Hamish's words trailed off. Beatrice was holding her face in her hands, quietly sobbing.

'What is it?' he asked. 'What's the matter?'

'I'm so sorry,' said Beatrice, wiping away her tears. 'When the people said you had changed, I refused to believe them. How could our Sir Hamish, the bravest young man in the kingdom, fall so far?' She held his hands and looked into his eyes. 'You were my Hamish, until that terrible day ... and I always dreamed you would come back to me. And now you have ... but your wits are truly addled, and your senses muddled.'

'No, my wits are okay, really,' said Hamish. 'I can crack jokes with the best of them. And my senses are doing fine ...' Then it dawned on him: she meant he had gone insane. 'I'm not crazy, unless you count leaping into a movie as the act of a crazy person ... but that's beside the point. It's just that ... I forget things. What exactly did happen on that terrible day?'

'Hamish! Don't play with me,' snapped Beatrice.

'Please tell me.'

'The king,' said Beatrice. 'He ... he ... I cannot ...'

'What?'

Beatrice stood abruptly and walked around to Hamish, rolling up his left sleeve. Hamish looked down at his arm and stifled a cry. A series of criss-cross scars ran all the way up to where his shirt covered his arm. It looked as though somebody had tried to toast the arm in a griller.

'Do you still want to see your cousin, the king?' hissed Beatrice.

'Um ... maybe not,' replied Hamish, swallowing a huge lump in his throat. He remembered now how the landlord had said he didn't want to see Hamish lose his head. And Old John had made a reference to Sir Hamish rotting in prison, where he was obviously tortured. Sir Hamish must have really got up King Ronald's nose. Enough for him to toast his cousin and nearly execute him. But that was all history now. He was here to defeat evil, and that meant stopping Dudley from poisoning the king.

Hamish looked over at Beatrice, still standing, a worried expression on her face. He looked down at his stained and dusty tunic. The people's champion was looking a bit past his use-by date. *Why the heck had Old John trusted me*? he wondered. *I'm a has-been, and I'm not even twenty-one!*

Has-been or not, he had to at least try. 'Look, Beatrice,' said Hamish. 'I don't want to see the king, but I have to see him. If you could please tell me which direction to get to the castle, and find me a sword ...'

Beatrice sat down opposite him and clutched his arms so hard it stung.

Yow! Please ...

She stared into his eyes, debating something in her head. Whatever it was, it caused her great distress. Tears rolled down her cheeks, and she whispered, 'Don't be so brave, my love. For once, be afraid, and everything will be so much easier ...'

'Afraid?' boomed Hamish, feeling a sudden rush of courage flow through his veins. 'I am Sir Hamish. The people's champion. They want to see me ride again, and I won't disappoint them. Give me a horse, get me my shield, I shall go to the castle and bash the doors down with my bare hands if need be.'

He stood abruptly and knocked his knees on the wooden table, buckling to the floor with the pain.

'Ow! Ow! Ow! I think I've decapitated my legs!'

'Take care!' laughed Beatrice, helping him up from the ground. 'The great hero has fought his battle for the day.'

'I'm just not used to my size, that's all,' said Hamish. 'You should try adding ten centimetres overnight.'

Beatrice looked at him intently again, the debate raging once more. This time she came to a decision, and said, 'It was destined that I come to the castle with you, and yet I still had half a mind ... All right. If you insist on going to the castle, then I am coming too.'

'No, no,' said Hamish. 'You're a simple washerwoman. This is my quest, it might get dangerous ...'

Beatrice slapped him on the shoulder, her eyes dark and furious. 'You always were a proud and stubborn man, but sooner or later you have to accept help. Look at you, knocking your knees without even facing an enemy. What if you meet a lair-goblin on the road?'

'Lair-goblin,' said Hamish. 'Exactly what is a lair-goblin?'

'Or a dragon-hag?' continued Beatrice, ignoring him. 'Or a fell-demon? Will you fight them with your knees? I think not. You never minded help in the old days ...'

'What old days?' asked Hamish.

She glared at him, her eyes ablaze with fury.

Oops. Maybe I've asked one question too many …

'You really do not remember the battles?' said Beatrice, her voice soft with menace.

'Um … er … would you believe me if I said I really, really, want to remember?'

Beatrice seemed to rise a few degrees in temperature.

Try again …

'Look, I seem to be doing this a lot lately,' said Hamish. 'I don't suppose if I asked you to remind me you would …'

That was the final straw. Beatrice started flinging crockery at Hamish's head, saying how dare he forget the day the goblin king was slain, or how dare he forget the night the sea-trolls were defeated, or how dare he … Hamish took cover, shouting back soothing words. He had no idea why she was so angry about the fact that he'd forgotten all his past glorious victories. Now was not the time to ask. Eventually she calmed down, and he agreed that he definitely needed her to come with him to the castle. Anything to stop her from throwing plates at him.

She looked at him, and a slow smile came to her face. 'The very first thing you'll need is a disguise,' she said, turning his face this way and that. 'And I have just the one in mind.'

Something tells me I'm not going to like this, thought Hamish, as Beatrice started busying herself looking for her disguise. She hummed happily, the earlier fire and rage gone. Hamish was glad she was on his side, because an angry Beatrice would be a very scary opponent.

Maybe I can do this, he thought. *Now that I have her help.*

He wondered when he'd ever get back to his life at Capra. Would this Vidz go on and on forever? Would he be stuck here? He put that thought out of his mind, concentrating on the Capra buildings, and the Capra people. He could see teachers, and students ... and Cushing. Who was he talking to? What was he planning now? And who was watching him?

10

Scene ten

Kaz and Bo are crouched in the garden outside the Principal's office, listening to a conversation taking place inside.

> BO
> (whispers)
> This is nuts. They're just talking about the football.

> KAZ
> Shh. Just listen, will ya?

She peers through the window, and we see that Cushing
is sitting with the Principal, MR ARBUCKLE. Bo joins
her to look inside. Mr Arbuckle is an old man, close to
retirement, but he is also very proud.

> CUSHING
> I've been talking to my friends. They say
> you've been unlucky with the horses lately.

> ARBUCKLE
> It's just a momentary blip. My luck will
> return.

> CUSHING
> Let's hope so.

Outside the window, Kaz and Bo exchange a confused
look. What are they talking about?

> CUSHING
> I was wondering ... have you considered our
> little scheme?

> ARBUCKLE
> Yes, I have, but I wonder if it is legal.

> CUSHING
> (angrily)
> I've already told you it's fine ...
> (changes his tone)
> Yes, I understand your concern. But you
> know it is perfectly safe, and it's a
> wonderful opportunity to increase the finances
> of the school ...

ARBUCKLE
But the rules are clear about investing the
school's money. And this is more like gambling.

CUSHING
(shouts)
It is not gambling! I've already told you that.

ARBUCKLE
Really, if you're going to be rude, then perhaps
you should leave.

Cushing stands abruptly.

CUSHING
Fine. I'll go ...

Arbuckle suddenly stands too, clutching desperately at
Cushing's arm.

ARBUCKLE
I'm sorry, I didn't mean to sound harsh.

Kaz and Bo are shocked by their Principal's behaviour.

ARBUCKLE
You won't let this interfere with our other
arrangement, will you?

CUSHING
I can't guarantee ... My friends are not very
patient people.

ARBUCKLE
Look, sit down. Have a drink. Why don't I
write a modest cheque out for, say, $50,000?

>   CUSHING
>   We agreed on $500,000.
>
>   ARBUCKLE
>   But that's almost all of the school's money.

Cushing sighs, and is about to turn.

>   ARBUCKLE
> $300,000!
>
>   CUSHING
>   Done.

Cushing smiles and sits, and Arbuckle opens a drawer
and pulls out a cheque book.

>   ARBUCKLE
>   And you guarantee that your scheme will
>   double this money?
>
>   CUSHING
>   It's as safe as if it was in a bank.
>
>   ARBUCKLE
>   Because if it fails ... it spells the end of Capra
>   High.

Outside the window, Kaz and Bo pull back, sneaking
away. When they are safely out of sight they run,
stopping in the street outside the school.

>   BO
>   What the heck was that all about?

KAZ

Do you have to ask? Cushing has some kind of
hold over Arbuckle. He's forcing him to give
over most of the school's money.

BO

Hang on, Kaz. He's the Principal.

KAZ

You saw what I saw.

BO

I don't know. There could be a good reason
why he wrote that cheque …

KAZ

Bo!

BO

They're teachers, Kaz. I mean, Arbuckle's our
Principal. He's, like, respected and all that.
Maybe we've got it wrong? You have to admit,
you hate Cushing's guts because of all your
family stuff.

KAZ

So?

BO

So, it might affect the way you see this.

KAZ

No way. Come round tonight. We have to work
out what to do next.

BO

Okay. I'll be there.

They separate. Camera stays on Kaz, who seems deep
in worry as she walks down the street.

11

Scene eleven

The beautiful castle of King Ronald.
So peaceful until...

'Aaaaaarrrrgh!'

'Really, Your Majesty. That's the third guard
you've thrown out the window today.'

'Then why don't I feel
any better?'

King Ronald looked more like a boy than a ruler. He always seemed to be young, even though he had the blood pressure of an old man. This was mainly because of all the tantrums he threw. Not to mention all the guards he threw as well. In fact, so legendary was the king's temper that the castle carpenters had built a special platform outside his window so that the guards could land safely and carry on with their duty: to serve the king … and occasionally be thrown out the window.

Ronald thumped the banquet table with his fist and shouted, 'I will not have my feast day ruined. I will not! I will not!'

He went redder and redder in the face, and his courtiers, who usually surrounded him closely, all took a step backwards. They had no intention of flying through the afternoon sunshine, even if there was a landing zone below. Only Lord Dudley stayed beside the ranting king. He was a tall, lithe man with a face that held deep shadows and dark secrets. All who knew Dudley feared him greatly. It was said that he once turned a cook into a pig for daring to serve up a cold meal. Such stories are always told in whispers in a castle, and most who heard this one laughed at it. Even so, none dared to cross the Lord Dudley.

As the king continued to rant and rave, Dudley removed a lace kerchief from his robes and sniffed gently on its lavender scent, a bored expression on his face. When at last the king had run the full course of his tantrum, the lord waved his hand at the cowering courtiers, who slunk out of the hall noiselessly.

'Still here, Dudley?' panted Ronald.

The tall man bowed low. 'I remain, as always, at Your Majesty's service.'

'You do not slink out like a sly rat when your king is in a temper?'

'Why should Your Majesty's moods frighten me?' said Dudley, smiling sweetly.

To most other observers, Dudley's smile was as pleasant as staring into the eyes of a snake, but to the king it was a sign that Dudley was still his faithful advisor who had helped him greatly through troubled times.

'That Hamish is a spoilsport!' shouted the king. 'I release him from prison as a gesture of goodwill and now look what he does!'

'Do not let the antics of your buffoon of a cousin trouble you, my lord,' said Dudley. 'He has lost all his powers ...'

'Yes,' said the king. 'The people's champion is nothing but a nanny's boy, but it troubles me to hear that he has murdered a peasant. He disrespects the royal name.'

'Ah ... yes,' said Dudley, adopting a troubled look. 'The death of any of Your Majesty's subjects is indeed a cause to mourn.'

'I won't have it, Dudley. I've been looking forward to my feast day for so long now. And Hamish is going to ruin everything. Do you know they will unveil a tapestry showing me hunting and killing a mighty stag?'

'Indeed,' said Dudley, seeing fit to bow low once more. 'And I have seen this tapestry. A fine likeness of Your Majesty.'

'I know what people are saying,' whined the king. 'That I have never been hunting in my life, let alone killed a stag. But that's because of my sickly constitution.'

'Who dares say such a thing about Your Majesty?' exclaimed Dudley. 'I shall have their head now! Don't they realise that you are a feeble man?'

'No, they don't,' pouted the king.

'Why, if you left the castle, you might die ...'

'I might.'

'That is why you need me to look after your kingdom for you.'

'That's right!' thundered the king.

The royal person slumped into his great chair, sighing loudly. All this thundering had quite exhausted him. He called for a hot drink of mead, then closed his eyes. Damn Hamish, thought King Ronald. Why did he have to ruin everything? Even when they were boys, it was always Hamish who was the better wrestler, or the better swordsman. Not that he ever beat his king. Nobody would dare beat the king at any game, but Hamish always had to show how strong he was before he deliberately lost. He didn't even have the courtesy to appear weak before His Majesty.

Ronald had always been jealous of his cousin. Hamish had been his strongest and bravest warrior. And then he'd started defeating all manner of evil creatures. Trolls, hags, demons, dragons ... The people cheered him loudly, when really they should have been cheering for Ronald. After all, King Ronald had absolute power, not this pipsqueak champion. The fame and adulation had gone to Hamish's head. He'd had this insane idea that Dudley was plotting some evil against his king. That was the last straw for

Ronald. Hamish was too big to throw out the window, so Ronald had thrown him into the dungeons. And what fun Dudley had had with the hero down there. He'd tortured Hamish, trying to find out if the rumours were true that the people's champion had help from a secret magic. In the end he nearly sent the poor fool mad.

The king clapped his hands together, and several guards came running.

'Arrest Hamish immediately,' he bellowed. 'Throw him into my dungeons until after the feast. It was a mistake to ever set him free in the first place.'

The guards bowed low, and were about to leave when Dudley spoke in a voice that dripped with honey but smelled of evil.

'If you permit it, Your Majesty, I should like to take charge of the arrest of Hamish. After all, you want to make sure it is done properly.'

'Yes, yes,' said the king. 'Make it so, Dudley. Make it so.'

And the mighty King Ronald left the hall, with the help of two guards. He paused at the doorway for a brief second to look pale and wan, then was gone. The head of the guards saluted Dudley. His name was Boris — a large man who ate more than his share at the guards' meal table, and tortured even more than his share of the prisoners in the dungeon.

'I shall send twenty men to arrest Hamish, my lord,' he said.

A brief, troubled look passed over Dudley's face, then he spoke. 'Very good. My spies have sent me reports that Hamish is in the north.'

Boris looked puzzled. 'North? But all reports I have say that Sir Hamish is in the south, my lord ...'

Dudley looked up, a fierce, evil anger in his eyes. 'Do you dare question me?'

Boris went pale with fear. He bowed low and said, 'You are infinitely wise, my lord.'

A brief smile crossed Dudley's lips. 'Yes,' he said. 'I am wise. Send the men north, then report to me. I have a little ... surprise in store for you.'

The head guard left quickly, glad for the moment that he hadn't been tossed out the window, but worried that Lord Dudley's 'surprise' might have something to do with the grunting and squealing of a porker named Boris.

12

Scene twelve

Hamish didn't know what felt more uncomfortable, the large bundle of lice-ridden straw Beatrice had strapped around his waist to make him look fatter, the scratchy linen dress he had been forced to wear, or the smell of sweat leaking from his fake hair. The king needn't bother lopping his head off, all the disgusting smells of Beatrice's disguise would do the job nicely.

So much for the rebirth of the people's champion. Hamish had imagined himself looking like a magnificent hero, not his mum! Beatrice was right, a disguise was a good idea. He just wished she could have thought of something a bit more impressive. Maybe this awful costume was her revenge on him for forgetting so much. It still puzzled him why she had been so angry. So what if he couldn't remember how many trolls and bogey-men he'd killed? Or *how* he'd killed them? He imagined he'd simply struck these lair-goblins through with his sword, 'Justice'. Of course, it would help if he still had his sword, and if he knew where to stick a lair-goblin. For a very brief second he contemplated asking Beatrice, then sanity took over and he said, 'Have you heard of the story of Toad from *Wind in the Willows*?'

'Who is Toad?' asked Beatrice.

Hamish smiled. 'He once wore a similar disguise. Let me tell you along the way.'

They set off on the dusty road towards the castle, with Hamish telling Beatrice the story of Toad and Ratty and Mole. It was a pleasant enough distraction as they walked in the sunshine, but once the story had finished the walk became long and uncomfortable. Hamish had to stop every now and then to scratch, or to adjust the straw-stuffing which kept twisting around his waist. And when he wasn't doing that, he was worrying about meeting up with some kind of nasty, maggot-infested *thing*. How could he kill a beast of evil? Throw his lice and fleas at it?

If only I had that sword, thought Hamish. He picked up a stout stick, imagining what it would be like to wield a huge, deadly weapon. Certainly his real self wouldn't have a chance of lifting it, but the Vidz-Hamish sure could swing it. He tried to remember what it was like, and a glimpse of a scene came to him. Swinging Justice, hearing it swish through the air, feeling it bite into an enemy, knowing the blade would be true. But the weirdest thing was that he didn't *see* the memory, he was *in it*.

Beatrice turned to him, and gasped with shock.

'What's wrong?' asked Hamish.

'Nothing,' said Beatrice, looking at the ground. 'You were ...' She was clearly shaken. 'What were you thinking, just now?' she asked.

'I was thinking about making a dragon-hag a few feet shorter with Justice!' boomed Hamish. *I was what? How the heck do I know about dragon-wagons, or hags, or whatever?*

'Ah,' said Beatrice. 'And how did you relieve the dragon-hag of its legs, Sir Champion?'

Parry! Feint! Thrust!

'You forget that dragon-hags have a long reach, Sir Champion!'

'And so does Justice, fair maiden!'

'Hamish ...' whispered Beatrice.

He stopped as suddenly as he'd started, breathing heavily, a stick in his hands. *What was that all about?* Hamish wiped his brow. 'I felt so powerful,' he said.

'You called me "fair maiden",' said Beatrice in a soft voice.

'I did?' said Hamish. 'Isn't that what you are?'

'I thought ...' started Beatrice, then she looked to the ground, crying.

'What ails you, Beatrice?'

'Nothing. I thought, just for a moment, that you might have started remembering ...' Hamish scratched his head. This was all getting too much for him. Remembering what? He didn't even know who he was anymore. Memories came to him that belonged to a character out of a movie. And *real* memories, too. He *knew* what it felt like to hold that sword. Knew how to use it, even. That was way too much to cope with, and now Beatrice wanted him to remember more. Memories were dangerous things!

'I don't remember anything else,' he said, sounding much harsher than he intended to.

Beatrice glared at him, a wild rage in her eyes, the same anger he had seen in the cottage. 'I was a fool,' she hissed. 'A fool to even think that you ... that we might ... Ah! Wasn't it always so? You always took the glory. Proud, arrogant champion! I hate you!'

And then she ran off into the woods, vanishing fast into the dense trees.

'Beatrice?' called Hamish. 'Come back!'

He had to go after her, soothe her anger, apologise, tell her he didn't mean it. Running as fast as his legs would carry him and flinging the ridiculous costume aside, Hamish set off after Beatrice. He bashed against trees and stumps, but what did he care? His true love was upset, crying, and it was all his fault ...

Wait a minute! True love? What am I thinking? It's ONLY A MOVIE!

This brief thought flashed through his mind, but he set it aside. This was real, this forest, that maiden, this quest. No other world made any sense, nothing else mattered.

13

Scene thirteen

Kaz and Bo are in Kaz's TV room, in the middle of a
discussion that is quickly turning into an argument. Bo
is lounging on a sofa, his usual laid-back self, but Kaz
paces up and down the room.

> KAZ
>
> But we have to do something, Bo. Cushing will
> make the whole school go bust.

> BO
>
> What can we do? We're just kids. As if we can
> stop a man like that.

KAZ
We go to the police.

BO
And tell them what? Come on, Kaz, you've
seen as many movies as I have. The kids go to
the police, tell them about the plot, the police
ask if the kids have evidence, the kids shrug …
Next scene, the kids are back out on the
street. We'd be wasting our time.

Kaz flops down next to Bo, furious, her legs jiggling, her
face seething with rage.

KAZ
I hate this! It's soooo frustrating!

Bo sits up and grabs a DVD from the table.

BO
Hey, let's just watch a vid, okay? What's
this one?

He reads the label on the DVD.

BO
'Vidz?' Never heard of it.

KAZ
Me neither.

BO
Then how did it get here?

Kaz leans forward and takes the DVD.

KAZ

Beats me. Let's play it and see what it's about.

BO

Probably some wildlife documentary ...

KAZ

Oh, please.

Bo puts the DVD into the slot. End on close-up of their
faces, watching, as the VIDZ VOICE explodes from the
screen.

VIDZ VOICE

Aaaaaaaaand ACTION!

'Forgive me, Beatrice. My mind... Perhaps Dudley's torture did change me?'

'What was that noise?'

'Quick, my love. Come inside this hut ...'

Hamish and Beatrice entered the hut. It was made up of planks, mud and thatching, and the doorway was an open hole. If the decor was bad, it was nothing compared to the smell.

Hamish instantly held his nose. 'Ugh! Who owns this place?' he said.

'Old John does ... or did,' answered Beatrice.

'Old John?' said Hamish.

He stared at Beatrice for a moment. Something was bothering him, a nagging thought. When he'd told Beatrice about Old John's sudden demise, she'd mentioned that she hardly knew the old beggar.

'How do you know this is Old John's hut?' he asked.

Beatrice turned a deathly shade of white. She looked this way and that, stammering, 'I ... er ... perhaps ...'

'Never mind,' said Hamish, waving his hand at her. 'We should look about, see if we can find something to connect Dudley to the plot.'

'No!' said Beatrice forcefully. 'Please, the old beggar is dead now. It would be disturbing his resting place ...'

'He died next to the well,' said Hamish, shaking his head. Why was she acting so strangely?

'But his spirit may look on.'

'Bah!' cried Hamish. 'What nonsense.'

He released the hold over his nose and was instantly hit by the stinking assault.

'Does anybody ever wash around here?' he exclaimed, beginning the search. Food scraps and bones were littered across the dirt floor, and there were patches of something unspeakably revolting on the walls. This hut was the perfume shop from hell. Beatrice stood by, a dark look on her face, as Hamish picked his way through the putrid mess. He stared at her, but she refused to lift a finger. Hamish the Hero wouldn't care about the smudges and smells, but right now he felt more like

Hamish the Squeamish. *First thing I do when I get back is have a long, hot bath. No. TWO long, hot baths!* His fingers touched something under the straw, just as he heard another noise outside the hut.

'There's someone out there for sure,' he hissed.

They both listened, but could only hear birds.

''Tis nothing but a lark building her nest,' said Beatrice, crossing her arms.

Hamish nodded, then dug deeper into the straw, wrapping his fingers around something soft. *I hope this isn't a dead cat!* He pulled out a small cloth bag, tied and held together with a golden seal. It most certainly was not the sort of thing Old John could have afforded.

'Whose seal is this, Beatrice?' asked Hamish.

He looked up to see that Beatrice now had her back to him and was over by the far wall.

'It is that of Lord Dudley,' she said flatly.

'How would you know? You haven't even looked at it,' said Hamish.

She didn't reply. He shrugged and broke the seal, opening the bag. It was filled with gold coins.

'A fool's ransom,' he said. 'Paid by the Lord Dudley to silence Old John. But it was money wasted, because the beggar told me about the plot. This is it, Beatrice. We have proof of our assassin.'

He stood, the bag still in his hand. It had been so easy. Maybe all Vidz were like this, offering up the clues for you. It was time to act. He set off for the door, then noticed that Beatrice hadn't moved.

'What is it now?' asked Hamish.

'So,' she said, 'you will take this proof to the king, and

accuse Dudley. Do you remember, perhaps, another time that you accused Dudley of plotting against his king?'

'Um, er ... if I said "No", would you start throwing things at me again?'

Beatrice sighed, and sat on a rickety wooden stool. 'It was the reason for your arrest last year, Hamish. I tried to stop you, but you wouldn't have it. Oh no, not the bold Sir Hamish. You had to blunder in and accuse Dudley in front of the entire court, where I could not help you.'

Where Beatrice couldn't help? But ... how would she have helped? Once again, Hamish weighed up whether he should ask the question or not, but since questions were dangerous things around this fierce maiden, he decided to try for an apologetic look instead.

'You don't recall that, either. Do you?' she asked.

'Like I said,' explained Hamish, 'Dudley tortured me in the dungeons ... I think it was in the dungeons. Whatever. He did horrible things and it ...'

Beatrice held up her hand. 'You went in alone against Dudley, when everyone knew in their whispers and nightmares that he held evil, magical powers. You went in knowing that you were the only man who could stop Dudley, but not without ... without ...'

Beatrice stood and gave the old stool a vicious kick. It bounced and rolled before hitting the wall and dislodging a wooden paling.

Nice strike, thought Hamish. Then he came to his senses. What had Beatrice been about to say? There was some kind of secret lurking here, but whenever it came up she went strange on him. Maybe she was waiting for him to remember it. She'd be waiting a long time.

'Why don't you just tell me what you want to say?' he asked.

'Enough,' cried Beatrice. 'From the moment you ran into my yard and hid in the washing, I had hoped that you would have the sense not to go on this fool's chase. Then when you were determined, I thought I could help you come back to who you were, to who we were. But it is in vain. Go then to the castle. I shall come too, because there is unfinished business for me there. A pact has been made, and now I must see it through.'

'Would you mind saying all that again?' asked Hamish, his head spinning. 'I didn't quite catch that bit after "Enough!"'

'Hamish!'

'Okay, okay. We'll go to the castle.'

Sheesh! Talk about sensitive. She ought to try taking on the role of a guy who had a heroic past with a strange, magical secret to it that he can't remember. It's exhausting!

He squared his shoulders and tried to be the manful Hamish that he looked like. Whatever happened, going to the castle was the right thing to do. 'If only I had my sword,' he said.

'No-one has seen it since that day,' whispered Beatrice.

'Then I shall fight with this,' shouted Hamish, grabbing an old straw broom.

Beatrice was about to say something further when her attention was distracted by a sound at the door. She turned and gasped, clutching the champion tightly on the arm.

The beast carries a takeaway snack into the hut.
Now it wants dinner!

'Begone, foul
creature!'

'Oh, for a real sword. Who shall help me now?'

What light is this?

The troll screamed a hideous cry, then ran from the hut, knocking out one of the walls in the process. Beatrice ran to the girl and boy the troll had dropped on the floor, lifting the girl up by her arms. Hamish, panting heavily from the fight, helped the boy to his feet.

'Are you all right?' asked the champion.

'Wh ... wh ... what ... what was ... THAT?' stammered the boy.

'Just a troll,' said Beatrice, matter-of-factly. 'Stupid creatures, mostly, but very strong. Oh, and they also eat people. Obviously he wasn't too hungry, otherwise ...'

'Okay,' said the girl, standing on her own now. 'We get the picture.'

Hamish looked at her. She talked differently to most of the people in this Vidz. The girl looked back at him, almost challenging him to say something. The two intruders were young, about Hamish's real age. Their faces were painted pure white, with bright red lips and dark blue eyelids. Both were dressed in outlandish costumes — bright tights with stars and moons glittering from the fabric, and quilted tunics with tiny bells sewn into the hems. There was something familiar about them, but Hamish didn't think much of it. He was so muddled with his own memories and Sir Hamish's memories that he couldn't tell who owned which anymore.

'What happened ... before?' asked the boy, his voice still shaking. 'With that light?'

'I was about to ask the same question,' said Hamish. 'It was like ... a flash going off, or something.'

The boy and girl exchanged quick glances, as Beatrice said, 'Pardon, my love? A flash, you say?'

'It's nothing, nothing,' said Hamish, blushing.

'What we saw was sunshine from the window,' said Beatrice with a smile. 'That is all. Trolls do not like direct sunshine. Now, tell us your names, young painted strangers.'

'My name is Zed,' said the girl. 'And this is my ... brother, Bee.'

Hamish regarded them suspiciously. What were they doing here in the woods at Old John's cottage? It was a long way from the road.

'Are you lost?' he asked.

'We came looking for ... er ... water,' said Bee.

The girl, Zed, had a strange look in her eyes, as if she was afraid of something. She moved nervously from one foot to the other. Bee, on the other hand, seemed to have relaxed from the ordeal, grinning broadly as if life itself were one big joke.

'Where are you headed?' asked Beatrice.

'The castle,' answered Zed.

'Well, we were, until that thing came along,' said

Bee. 'We are to play for the king himself. We shall make him laugh and cry.'

'You both look so young,' said Beatrice.

'Er ... have you not heard of us?' cried Zed. 'Our fame stretches far and wide throughout the land. We have entertained at royal courts before.'

Beatrice placed her strong arm around the girl's shoulder and smiled warmly. 'No need to be offended, my little star. We are merely curious, that is all. So, you say you are off to the castle? You are in luck. We are heading that way ourselves. Join us. Hamish here will fight off any hungry trolls with a stray broom or two.'

Hamish shot Beatrice a sharp look. What was she doing? Their mission to the castle was top secret. Beatrice ignored Hamish's look and continued speaking to the girl in a soothing, warm voice. 'This merriment you have planned for the king. How many travelling players would the castle be expecting?'

Hamish grinned. So that was what she was up to. Entering the castle as two washerwomen was always going to be difficult, but entering as part of a performing troupe was a much easier prospect.

'The guards will only be expecting players,' said Zed. 'No number has been mentioned. Why? Do you perhaps need a way into the castle tonight?'

Beatrice laughed heartily and said, 'Come, let us see what costumes you have in your bag of tricks.'

Scene fifteen

The guards at the castle gate were in a jovial mood. Tomorrow would be the Great Feast, and that always meant the odd plate of tasty food coming their way. The head guard, Boris, patted his enormously fat stomach and grinned broadly.

'I can hardly wait, my friends,' he said with glee. 'Roast bird, roast meat, roast vegetables ...'

'And roast guard if we stray from our post,' said a young sharp-eyed guard.

The others laughed, nodding at the miserable lot of

a castle guard — left to sit in the dark, manning a lonely sentry post while the rest of the court had fun. They gave Boris a sly look. The head guard would not normally be seen on such paltry duty. Word was that Boris had somehow annoyed the Lord Dudley and this guard duty was his punishment. Boris had joked that he wanted to share a story or two with the men at the gates, but in his many little naps he'd been heard to mutter in his dreams, 'Not a pig! I don't want to be a pig.'

Boris looked at them, and seemed to be able to read their thoughts. 'As I said, lads, being on duty for the feast makes a change from guarding prisoners.'

'Now, Boris,' said Mikka, the sharp-eyed guard. 'I heard you had great sport in making the prisoners dance a merry tune ...'

'Aye,' said Boris. 'I had my fun.'

'Tell us some stories,' said one of the younger guards.

Boris shook his head. 'I'll let the travelling players tell the stories, my lad. They will have happier tales than my own. But perhaps one day you shall come down to the cells with me and have some sport yourself.'

The young guard nodded eagerly, but the other guards who'd been in the dungeons shuddered slightly. The cells were a dark and horrible place.

At that moment a cart laden with an enormous slain ox arrived at the gates, and Boris could barely contain himself as it was wheeled into the castle grounds. 'Think of how much meat you'd get from that one, my lads.'

'Have you heard, Boris?' said Mikka, looking slyly over at the fat guard. 'Your favourite prisoner has been up to no good again.'

'If you mean Hamish, then I have heard. I would have had him in my dungeon again, but some had other plans ...'

'Do you speak of intrigue and plotting?' asked Mikka innocently.

'Hush,' said Boris, looking about nervously. 'Such talk could see you end up grunting at the trough with a wee pink tail. The Lord Dudley has mysterious ways. If he wants to march soldiers north to find a man in the south, far be it from me to question him. All I know is that Hamish is a traitor.'

'So says the Lord Dudley,' whispered Mikka.

'You are either very brave or very foolish, young Mikka,' said Boris.

'I like to speak the truth,' said Mikka.

Boris stared hard at the young guard, then said, 'And I like to celebrate a feast. So let us continue with the party mood, my friends, and stop all this talk of politics.'

The conversation quickly changed to the weather, a safe enough topic after the dangerous talk of treason and betrayal. Boris stood up to stretch, and noticed a strange party of travellers approaching the gates from the south road. They were dressed in what appeared to be costumes. Two had their faces painted white, and they were leading an old donkey laden with boxes and suitcases. The other two were dressed as outlandish clowns, with coloured hair and bright clothing. Boris sighed. This would be the travelling players. He crossed his arms, waiting until the strangers were within earshot before shouting, 'Who seeks entrance to the castle?'

'An excellent afternoon to you, my good man,' shouted Zed in a theatrical voice. 'We have come to ...'

'I know, I know,' said Boris wearily. 'You have come to entertain the king. Well, you'd better be funnier than the last lot, or you'll wind up entertaining the rats in His Majesty's dungeon.' Boris turned to the other guards and shouted, 'Open the gates!'

'No need to bellow,' moaned Mikka as he unlocked the castle gates. 'We're right next to you.'

The other two guards helped to open the heavy gates, and the party of performers entered. Boris watched them closely as they passed him. Something was not right. He couldn't put his finger on the problem, but something about the clowns bothered him.

'Halt!' yelled Boris.

'Have I seen you before, clown?'

'I am but a humble clown, Sir Guard. I come with no mischief, except the mischief of fun and laughter.'

'Let them pass!'

16

Scene sixteen

Hamish sat in the corner of the courtyard trying to block out the sounds of Zed and Bee rehearsing. At any other time he would have been entertained by the acrobatic antics of the two travelling players, but he could not shake off a powerful feeling of doom. Something was about to go wrong, he just knew it. Ever since they'd entered the castle and he'd been questioned by Boris, his mood had sunk lower and lower.

Beatrice noticed this, and took him aside while the two performers continued their rehearsal. 'What is it, Hamish? You have not spoken for an hour.'

'That guard at the gate,' stammered Hamish. 'He ... I ... I remember him ... Oh, Beatrice. I don't know if I can do this. I close my eyes and I can see that prison ...' He held onto Beatrice's arm for support as the horrible images of the king's prison came flooding into his head — the sneers on the guards' faces as they served him his slops for dinner, the sting from their whips, the rank odour of the disgusting cells, and most of all, the look of hatred on Boris's face.

The real-Hamish struggled to speak reason in his head, to say it was never real, that it had only happened in the movie. But the Vidz-Hamish shivered as he remembered every bite of the whip, every nip from the rats. It was too much to bear. Hamish was being swamped by a thousand ugly memories. He couldn't think straight, he couldn't breathe. Everywhere around him was danger. Every person around him was an enemy.

'We have to get out of here!' he cried, causing the two performers to stop and stare at him. 'Yes, yes,' Hamish shouted at them. 'Sir Champion is mad. He is addled. Go now and tell Dudley ...'

Beatrice had to clamp her hand over his mouth until he stopped staring wildly and breathing like a demented man. He looked at her, and thought that for a moment he could see a glow of white light around her face.

'Beatrice,' he whispered. 'That light ...'

'Light?'

'Your face ...?'

'Yes, Hamish. What do you see? Please tell me ...'

He stared hard at her, but it seemed that the longer he looked, the more the light faded, until there was nothing but the dull afternoon greyness around them.

'Nothing,' he said. 'I saw nothing.'

Beatrice's shoulders sagged, and her face seemed to set in stone. 'Rest here,' she said. 'I shall get you some water.'

'Yes, please,' said Hamish. 'And a peanut butter sandwich ...'

'A what?'

'I mean, cheese and bread.'

Beatrice stood, looking at him warily. 'You are close to where they tortured you,' she said. 'So your mind is weaker, I suppose.' Then she sighed. 'I had hoped it would be different. This castle is an evil place. We are both close to where our lives were torn apart.' Beatrice turned quickly, and left the courtyard.

Torn apart? My life and hers? But what did Dudley do to Beatrice? Or ... what did Hamish do to her?

Hamish stared at the two players to take his mind off riddles. There was something about them — he'd first noticed it in Old John's hut. What was it again? He racked his brain, but it seemed that every spare ounce of his energy was taken up trying to keep the horrifying memories of the dungeon out. Zed and Bee had stopped rehearsing by now, and were looking in Hamish's direction.

'Why have you stopped?' he asked.

'Um,' said Bee. 'Can we talk to you?'

Hamish nodded, and the travelling players came over. 'What is it?'

'Well,' said Zed, fidgeting nervously. 'You kinda seem familiar to us ... and we wondered ...'

'Wondered what?'

'If you were,' continued Bee, 'you know. If you were ... different, like us.'

'Different?' said Hamish.

He tried to concentrate on what they were saying, but an overwhelming sense of betrayal and suspicion washed over him. This was the castle, and it was full of plots and evil. What had these two meant by 'different'? A voice struggled inside his head, trying to tell him to listen, saying strange words like 'Capra' and 'Video', but he shut it out. He was Sir Champion, and he knew a couple of plotters when he saw them. These two were up to no good.

He stood quickly, towering over the two youngsters and bellowed at them to 'Begone!' They ran from the courtyard in fright. Suddenly all the energy in Hamish's legs seeped out. He sat down in some straw, holding his head.

What is happening to me?

He closed his eyes and visions came to him. Strange images: a dark night in the castle grounds, Beatrice at his side. She looks so different. There is a bright glow about her. A white light. 'Maiden,' he is saying to her. 'Maiden, I shall go to my king unarmed.' Beatrice looks alarmed at this. 'But, Hamish, the Crystal's power,' she says. 'You may need it.' He can see the fear on her face, and he strokes it with his rough fingers. 'Don't worry,' he whispers. 'I have the power of truth ...' And now ... now he is asking her for something ...

Hamish sat up with a fright. *What was that all about*? He looked around the courtyard as if he was seeing it for the first time. Where were Zed and Bee? Where was Beatrice? The afternoon had almost faded away by now, and a chill was in the air. Hamish stumbled over to the stables and lay down in the straw, pulling a velvet cape from the travelling players' costume box over himself for warmth. He felt exhausted, drained of all energy. He had to sleep. Get away from all this. Sleep ...

As the light bled from the day, the bold Sir Hamish fell into a fitful dream.

Scene seventeen

Others were busy in the darkened castle.

The travelling players discuss a plot.

What twist do they hatch?

The guard, Mikka.

And elsewhere ...

Beatrice has an unexpected visitor.

'I have done as you asked, my lord. Now do you have my light?'

'You shall have your precious trinket, maiden. But first I have another task for you ...'

18

Scene eighteen

He was being chased through the night by a dark, mysterious knight who swung a huge sword. Again and again the knight lunged with the sword, until Sir Hamish fell to the ground, his face in the cold mud, the knight's boot on his back pinning him to the ground. Struggling with all his strength, Sir Hamish pushed himself free and rolled over. He reached out with his hands and clawed at his enemy's visor, trying to lift it. 'Show me your face!' he shouted. Was it Dudley? Was it one of those accursed players? Was it the king? He finally managed to lift the visor, and gazed at last at his enemy's face. But it was only a boy. A frightened boy with a bewildered look on his face.

Sir Hamish woke in a cold sweat, his heart racing at a mad pace, his hair matted across his forehead. What was this dream he'd had? Why would his enemy be a child? And who was this strange-looking boy? He seemed somehow familiar.

Blinking a few times, Sir Hamish tried to accustom his eyes to the gloomy atmosphere inside the stables. A faint glimmer of light came from a brazier that burned outside in the courtyard. After a few minutes he could make out shapes inside the stables. Was that dark figure near the foot of his bed Beatrice, or a bale of straw?

'Is that you?' he whispered.

A voice answered him, but it wasn't Beatrice. It was harsh and cold, a voice from beyond the grave.

'Hamish,' it moaned.

'Who goes there?' cried Hamish.

'You must listen ...'

The dark figure at the foot of his bed moved towards him, and Hamish tried to scramble to his feet.

'Go away! Go away! Help!'

'You must listen,' said the voice.

Hamish stopped, and this time he did listen. He knew that voice. 'Old John?' whispered Hamish.

'There is danger ...'

'Don't come any closer. I'm warning you,' he hissed.

The dark figure laughed, a gloomy, sad sound that echoed around the courtyard outside. 'I come to warn you,' it said. 'There is danger all around you. You must save the king. The assassin walks ... even now as we speak ... he moves about the castle plotting his evil plan. That which is dear to the king will be his undoing. Understand this ... that which the king holds dear and true will kill him!'

'What?' said Sir Hamish, trying to understand this ghostly riddle. 'What do you mean?'

But the ghost had finished speaking, and it swept away into the darkness, blending into the shadows. Hamish didn't wait to see if it would return with any more messages. He threw the cape aside and ran as fast as his legs would carry him.

19

Scene nineteen

'So, the great hero has seen a ghost?'

'Hamish is still strong, my lord.
What if he sees through the plot?'

'Do not worry. I have a surprise
for our champion tomorrow.'

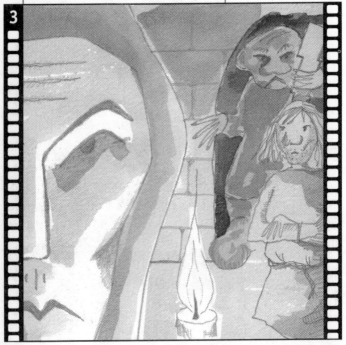

20

Scene twenty

Hamish ran like a madman, his arms out in front of him, his fingers clawing at the night air. Round blind corners, down slippery stone stairways and through narrow archways, until he came to a well-lit courtyard. It was then that he hit a soft object and landed flat on his bottom.

'Oh ...' moaned Hamish.

'Oh ...' moaned another voice beside him.

'Beatrice?'

'Hamish?'

'Beatrice,' cried Hamish, crawling towards her. 'I have seen a horror ... hold me. Please.'

He felt her warm, soft arms surround him as he lay his head on her chest. She soothed him with her sing-song voice until his heart stopped racing and his breath came in easy, slow rhythms.

'I saw ... I saw the ghost of Old John. He told me, "That which the king holds dear will be his undoing."'

'Hush now,' crooned Beatrice.

'Oh, my love,' said Hamish. 'I cannot live without you. I cannot breathe, I cannot think ... Please, stay by my side forever.'

'Hamish,' said Beatrice softly, 'you called me "my love".'

Hamish sighed. 'Yes,' he said. 'I'm so sorry, Beatrice. I have treated you so badly. After the king had me in his prison ... I abandoned everything.'

'It is all in the past now ...'

'No,' said Hamish. 'I remembered something. You asked me to remember, and I did.'

'What?'

'It was you ... and me. Before I accused Dudley the first time. I asked you for something ...'

'Yes?' whispered Beatrice. 'And it was ...?'

'It was a ... a ... No. I'm sorry. It's all gone now.'

Beatrice stood, letting Hamish fall to the cobblestones.

'Ow!'

She paced back and forth, hitting the walls with the palm of her hand, muttering under her breath. 'You took something from me,' she said, anger in her voice. 'From *us*! You were so close just now, Hamish. So close ...'

'Why is it so important that I remember?' asked Hamish. 'Couldn't you tell me instead?'

'No!' shouted Beatrice. 'Telling you will not bring back what you took. You *must* remember. And if you don't ...'

'And if I don't ... what?'

She stopped pacing and stood over him. 'Hamish, listen. I came to this castle to finish a deal. I am close to the end, close to getting the one thing I desire above all other things. But even now, my heart cries for you. So ... so run, Hamish. Run while you still have a chance.'

'What are you talking about? I have to save my king ...'

'Why? He imprisoned you. He tortured you.'

Hamish waved his arm, as if that were of no consequence to him. 'He is my king,' he said with pride, his chest swelling, his whole body seeming to grow stronger with each word he spoke. 'He is my king, and I am still his champion. It is my duty.'

'Then you are a fool,' whispered Beatrice.

Hamish stared at her. He couldn't work out her strange shifts of mood. Then it hit him. She talked of a deal, one which she obviously did not feel comfortable with. 'What deal have you made?' he asked.

Beatrice didn't answer. Instead she looked around at the courtyard they were in. 'Do you know this courtyard?' she asked.

He looked. It seemed the same as all the other courtyards he'd run through that night. Then a memory came to him, the same memory he'd had earlier about

Beatrice. 'It was here,' he said. 'We talked here before I was arrested ...'

Beatrice nodded. Hamish closed his eyes. He had felt so alone that night. Beatrice wanted to help, but he refused. He thought he would be stronger without her. He was wrong. Why couldn't he see that? And now? Hadn't he learned anything? It was Beatrice who had helped him get here. Her love. Not his own strength, or cleverness. Just simple love.

'You loved me back then,' whispered Hamish. 'You told me to take Justice with me when I confronted Dudley. But I said I would not ...'

Hamish suddenly clutched the leather pouch that he wore around his neck, removing the rusted metal disc from it that he'd offered the landlord as payment for his ale. That would have been a foolish thing to do — this metal disc was worth more than all the gold in the land, now that he remembered what it was for. He rushed to a far wall of the courtyard, placing the disc into an indentation in one of the large stones. It fitted perfectly. Hamish pushed on the stone, and it fell completely into the wall, creating a huge cavity. He reached into the hole with his hand and pulled out a long, weathered sword in a scabbard.

'Justice,' he whispered. 'Now I am truly back.'

He drew the mighty sword. Images came to him, of Justice defeating huge trolls, of Justice cutting down goblins and other unspeakable horrors, all the while glowing white as the sun. But there was another light, now that he thought of it. Another light that glowed next to him. A Crystal ...

'You,' whispered Hamish, looking over at Beatrice. 'You are the Crystal Maiden.'

'Yes,' said Beatrice.

'Together. Of course ... we defeated evil together!' Hamish slapped his forehead. 'How could I have been so stupid? We were a *team*. That is why you were so angry in your cottage. I'd forgotten that you acted in secret with me. *You* are my magic ...'

'And now you are alone,' said Beatrice, her voice hoarse.

'Alone?' said Hamish.

'Your sword once glowed with the Crystal's magic. I gave it that magic, so that we were bound always. Justice and the Crystal, until that night you ...'

'I remember! I asked you to give me the Crystal! So you wouldn't interfere. And you did ... I've done it, Beatrice. I've remembered.'

'Yes,' said Beatrice, a bitter look on her face.

'Well,' said Hamish, feeling very proud of himself. 'Aren't you glad now? I remembered about the Crystal.'

Beatrice shook her head. 'I trusted you that night. You were my love. My champion. I trusted you and you took my Crystal. Can't you see yet? Don't you understand? You stand so proud because you remember what happened, but where is my light now? My Crystal? What good is your memory?'

He was shocked by the anger in her face. All this time he thought she was his love, yet she secretly hated him. And all because of the magic Crystal ... that Dudley took. Yes, he saw that now. When he was tortured in the dungeon. He could see Dudley standing over him, a small, shiny bauble in his hands and a triumphant grin on his face. Dudley took the Crystal.

'Dudley has it,' he said.

Beatrice let out a moan, as if the air had been knocked out of her. She hung her head and said, 'For so long I have hoped that maybe Dudley had been lying to me. But now I know. That evil man really did torture you and take the Crystal while you lay half-dead in the dungeon. All through this journey I had hoped in vain that you'd remember where it was, that it was hidden somewhere safe. Now I have no choice but to do what Dudley has asked of me. At least he promises to give it back.'

'He what?' said Hamish, staring at her.

'Run, Hamish,' said Beatrice, her voice flat. 'Run now. This is a trap. Everything. Old John is no ghost. He never died. It was a trick to send you to me. And I am but another part in the trickery. That which the king holds dear? It is when they shall toast Ronald's good health with wine at the feast tomorrow. This is Dudley's final request of me, to poison my king, but this is more than getting rid of Ronald. This is about making it appear that the people's champion is the poisoner, Hamish. You. This is ridding the land of the one force that could oppose Dudley. And I must help him because he has promised to return my Crystal ... my life. Have you any notion of what it is like to be without your essence?'

Hamish nodded. He had a strong feeling of being cut off, away from his home, of drifting in another world. He wasn't sure where it came from, but the face of that boy in his dream seemed to be connected to it. And now he was alone again. Beatrice, the Crystal Maiden, who had fought in secret by his side for so long, had cut him off. Sold him out to Dudley. Yet even now she was giving him a chance to run.

'I am the people's champion,' he said. 'I do not run.'

'You are a proud fool to the end,' said Beatrice bitterly.

Hamish sighed, staring at his one-time companion. How had it come to this? He was wondering what to do next when the sudden sound of running feet filled the air. Before he had time to look around for somewhere to hide, guard rushed into the courtyard, their spears glinting in the orange light of the brazier, their faces grim with determination. At their side were the two travelling players, Zed and Bee, fear tingling their eyes. The tall young guard from the gates seemed to be leading the pack, and it was this man that Hamish rushed, Justice held high, swinging with a mighty stroke.

'For my king!'

How long could Mikka withstand Justice's stroke?

'Stop! Sir Hamish. Listen. We mean no harm. These guards are loyal to you ...'

The young guard knelt at Hamish's feet, laying his sword on the ground. 'Sir Hamish,' he said, 'I am Mikka. I offer you my fealty. These travelling players have only done as I bid them. They have led me to you because dark forces are at play. There are those within this castle who would have you dead. You are the people's champion. I still remember the day you rode into our village after destroying the green dragon ... I shall not let you die.'

'What do you say?' asked Hamish. 'You ask for my blessing.'

'Yes, Sir Hamish,' said Mikka. 'The people need you again. The Lord Dudley has a stranglehold on the land. He covers it in darkness and fear, and our king cannot see his evil ways.'

The guards who surrounded Hamish all dropped to their knees, bowing their heads. They spoke to him, saying, 'We need you, Sir Hamish,' and 'We will follow you to the end.' Hamish looked at their faces, and a powerful warmth filled his body. Beatrice stirred beside him, and he saw that she was crying. Silvery tears ran down her cheeks.

'Oh, Hamish,' she said, waving her hand at the men. 'This was why I loved you in the first place. You inspire the people. They know there is goodness in your heart. I only wish ... that my own heart was as good ...'

'But it is, my love,' said Hamish. 'You know that you are truly good. Even now you go against Dudley and warn me to leave the castle. Join me again, Crystal Maiden.' He held out his hand to her.

'But I have no magic, no power ...'

'I need you,' he whispered. 'What good is your Crystal to you if you win it back by doing Dudley's evil bidding?'

Beatrice hung her head. Hamish was right. The Crystal was a magic for fighting evil, not conspiring with evil. She belonged here on the side of goodness. Taking hold of Hamish's hand, Beatrice nodded her head and said, 'We will stand together again.' A mighty cheer erupted in the courtyard. Hamish felt as if he'd grown an extra yard in height. How could he fail now? He was surrounded by the loyalty of friends and the love of this maiden. He'd been a fool to think he could do this alone. That had only led to his downfall last time. Now it would be different. He would be part of ... a word came to him ... a strange word. *Crew*. He wondered what this word meant, yet at the same time he *knew* what it meant.

Crew, buddy. Movie crew, Vidz crew, this crew right here. A team of friends who go all the way to win.

That voice. He'd heard it before.

It's me, Hamish. The kid in the dream, except I'm real. So, come on, Sir Champion, it's time we kicked some evil bottoms in this Vidz!

Sir Hamish smiled. The secret knowledge of who he was gave him strength. 'Will you follow me?' he asked the host in the courtyard. 'Will you help me defeat Dudley once and for all?'

'Yes,' they called.

He could feel Beatrice squeeze his hand, and his heart filled with pride.

'These are dangerous times,' said Hamish. 'We shall need courage. We shall need strength. You, Mikka, take these men back to their posts and await the moment of truth. During the feast you shall hear the signal from the travelling players. Then I shall need your allegiance. Beatrice, you and the travelling players come with me to the Great Hall. We have some planning to do. There is no time to be lost!'

The guards ran from the courtyard, a new hope springing in their hearts. And as they left, Hamish thought he could detect a whisper among the guards, the same phrase repeated over and over. 'The people's champion has returned!'

The strange alliance of painted performers, handsome hero and mysterious maiden headed towards the Great Hall, grim determination showing on their faces.

'Can Dudley use the Crystal against us?' asked Hamish, linking his arm with Beatrice's.

'No,' she said. 'The true magic of the Crystal is awesome indeed. Not even Dudley would dare use its powers. The pure white light would shatter him like, well, tinkling crystal. Only I can use it. But of course, its magic is nothing unless I am joined with it.'

Hamish nodded, deep in thought. 'Then how did you make that white flash in Old John's cottage?'

Beatrice laughed. 'That was just a trick,' she said. 'A little bit of puff and froth. Nothing more.'

'Oh, said Hamish, sighing. 'I had hoped ...'

'I'm sorry,' said Beatrice. 'This will not be easy. Lord Dudley will unleash all his evil against us when he learns I have crossed him.'

'I know,' sighed Hamish.

Zed and Bee caught up with them, placing their young arms around the two champions of good.

'So, what's the plan?' asked Zed.

'Plan?' said Hamish. 'Mm, I have a few tricks in mind. They might be old, but I bet no-one around here has seen them before.'

The travelling players started laughing, slapping Hamish on the back. 'This is going to be so much fun,' they said.

Oh yes, thought Hamish. *We're coming to the final reel of this movie. And what a climax I have in mind!*

Scene twenty-one

As dawn came, the good folk of the castle went about their business preparing for the big moment. Food was cooked, tables laid and guests welcomed at the gates. The king's brothers and sister, princes and princesses of their own castles, arrived first. Then came his aunts and uncles, then his many, many cousins.

Some seemed bored by the prospect of a feast, others resigned, and others excited by the smells that wafted from the great kitchen.

Huge fires were stoked at the cook's shouted orders.

Serving women and men rushed about at great speed, wary of the cook's notorious temper, carrying boards of meat and other delights for the king's feast. A great table ran along the back wall of the kitchen, and it was here that the enormous trays were set, including several which each held fifty goblets of wine for the king's toast. Two guards with huge shields and spears stood by the goblets, posted there to make sure that no-one tampered with the king's wine. A serving wench moved about behind them, tapping one on the shoulder, then the other. The two guards turned towards each other, their shields clashing.

'Stand back, fool,' cried the first guard.

'No, you stand back!'

There was a clatter and a crash as the guards tussled over who would give way. Eventually the guards' spears became locked together, swinging through the air and knocking a tray of goblets from the table.

'Imbeciles!' shouted the cook, pushing the guards away from the mess. 'Get out of my kitchen.'

'But ... we are to stand here ...'

'Do you wish to be broiled over my stove?' screamed the cook.

The guards made their way out of the kitchen, and a bevy of workers began mopping the floor, setting the goblets right again and refilling them. They were too busy to notice that one of the wenches was reaching over the tray, pouring a dark liquid into each goblet from a leather pouch. When she was done, she scampered out of the kitchen.

22

Scene twenty-two

The Crystal Maiden, disguised as a wench, runs from the kitchen and heads towards the Great Hall, where everyone is seated and the travelling players are about to begin the performance. But as she reaches the corridor leading to the Hall, a menacing presence steps out to block her way.

'Good lady, you have done what I asked?'

'Yes, the king's wine is poisoned.'

'Good. Hamish will try to save the day. I will accuse him. *Then*, maiden, you shall have your trinket back.'

23

Scene twenty-three

Inside the Great Hall, His Majesty King Ronald was enjoying the antics of the travelling players. They were more amusing than the usual lot, with different acrobatics and a strange, almost otherworldly humour. The king was happy: with these players opening the show, his feast day was shaping up to be a very pleasant diversion from the humdrum of castle life.

'It is a pity that the Lord Dudley is not here to enjoy the japes these players make,' said Ronald. 'He needs all the diversion he can get. He is so serious ...'

Suddenly the enormous wooden doors at the far end of the Hall were flung open, and the king looked up to see Dudley enter the feast. The Lord Dudley strode down the middle of the Hall, completely ignoring the magnificent new tapestry above the doorway that depicted Ronald hunting down a stag. Ronald pouted. Surely Dudley could stop for one second and see how handsome his king looked? Was it too much to ask? The players were in the middle of some foolery when the Lord Dudley nearly knocked them over. The crowd of assembled onlookers gasped.

The king smiled. Trust Dudley to annoy the people. The fools probably believed that nonsense about him having evil powers. He was just a counsellor, that was all. His Majesty looked around the Great Hall, at the long tables that lined each wall. Every single brother, sister, cousin, aunt and uncle from his miserable family was there — all except Hamish. For a brief moment King Ronald felt a tinge of anger. Those fools of guards had failed in capturing his fourth cousin.

'Your Majesty,' said Lord Dudley as he arrived at the royal table. King Ronald offered his ring, never once taking his eye off the travelling players. It was just as well they had stepped out of Dudley's way. Rumour or not, it would be a shame to see these fine young folk turned into snorting pigs.

The players finished their act and the king threw a rose onto the floor as a token of his appreciation.

The wine was carried in on massive trays for the royal toast, and the king smiled to himself. 'Now will they show how much they love me,' he muttered.

The Lord Dudley rose to his feet and shouted across the vast hall. 'My lords, courtiers and assembled good folk, let us now drink to the health of His Majesty, King Ronald the Great.'

The king picked up a goblet, but slammed it down immediately. 'It's dirty,' he cried. 'You have this one, Dudley, I'll have yours.' A great cheer rose through the hall, and each and every one of the assembled guests raised their goblets enthusiastically and drank. They wanted their king to notice their loyalty, so they drank until their cups were dry ... all except for one.

The Lord Dudley held his still full goblet of wine, staring at the king, who also had not taken a drop.

'Drink with me, Dudley,' said Ronald.

He raised his goblet, and Dudley raised his, both men throwing back their heads to wild cheers from the crowd. When he had finished, King Ronald banged his empty goblet onto the wooden table, but was alarmed to notice that Dudley placed a full goblet next to his.

'Dudley?' said the king. 'You did not drink.'

'No, Your Majesty. I ... I ...'

The king tried to focus on what Dudley was saying, but his head started spinning and his vision grew faint and blurry. What was that thundering noise in his ears? Why did his head feel so large and heavy? How could the room spin so?

He tried to reach out to Dudley, who seemed pleased about something, but his arms felt thick and heavy. As he slumped in his seat, King Ronald could faintly hear a voice calling in the distance, shouting out some crazy message that just didn't make sense.

'Guards! Guards! Come at once! King Ronald has been poisoned!'

Then all went black.

24

Scene twenty-four

The second that Hamish heard Dudley's cry, he rushed into the Great Hall, Justice strapped to his side.

'There he is,' shouted the Lord Dudley, pointing at Hamish. 'There is the man who has poisoned our king.' But nobody answered Dudley's cry, nobody rushed to arrest Hamish. Dudley looked around the Great Hall for support, and was astonished to see that all the royal family, all the courtiers and all the good folk of the castle had their heads on the tables in front of them as if they were dead.

'Have I poisoned every single courtier, Dudley?' asked Hamish as he walked slowly towards his enemy.

'You have poisoned the king. And if you haven't already poisoned the guards, then they shall throw you in prison,' shouted Dudley. 'Guards! Guards! Come!'

A clatter of spears and a clanging of shields was heard as a dozen or so guards came running towards the Great Hall. Hamish nodded towards the travelling players. Zed and Bee rushed to each side of the wooden doors, waiting for the guards to enter the hall. As the last guard dashed through the doorway, Zed and Bee pulled on two cords that hung from the tapestry, sending the enormous cloth picture down onto the heads of the guards. They were smothered by the glorious vision of their king.

'Seize him!' shouted Dudley to another dozen guards who had rushed in from the entrance behind the king's table.

These men surrounded Hamish, wary of the great champion, their spears at the ready. Hamish backed away slowly, his eyes locked on his enemies. Closer and closer moved the guards, until they had reached the centre of the Hall. Finally Sir Hamish stopped and smiled at the hapless guards who stood before him with spears quivering.

But what is this above their heads?

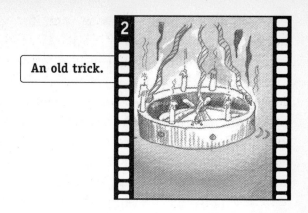

An old trick.

Trapped!

Zed and Bee turned to each other and clapped their palms together above their heads. Hamish noticed this out of the corner of his eye and paused.

Did they just do a high five? He shook his head. Now was not the time to wonder. He had to concentrate on being Sir Hamish. This battle wasn't over yet.

'You shall not escape that easily,' shouted the Lord Dudley, purple with rage. 'More guards! More guards!'

To his delight, more guards did enter the Great Hall, led by the cruel Boris.

'Players!' called Hamish. 'Blow your trumpet!'

Bee ran to where their theatrical props lay and pulled out a long trumpet, which he blew with all his might. Within seconds Mikka and his loyal guards burst in through the windows, surrounding Boris's men. They had been hiding on the landing-zone platform built for King Ronald's folly of tossing guards out the window.

'Now, now,' said Hamish, looking at the two sets of guards. 'This is an interesting predicament.'

Dudley looked to Boris and shouted, 'Arrest Hamish!'

'Wait!' yelled Mikka. 'Hear Sir Hamish out, first.'

Boris scratched his chin, looking warily at Dudley before folding his arms. 'Perhaps one man poisoned would be normal,' he said. 'But a whole court? I will give you ten seconds to say what you have to say, Hamish.'

'You fool!' shouted Dudley. 'You dare cross me again? This man has poisoned his king ...'

'Why do you speak so readily of poison?' asked Hamish.

Dudley shifted his eyes about, and as he glanced at his full goblet a niggling doubt formed in his mind. He clutched at his velvet tunic. 'Look at him for yourself!' he spluttered, pointing at the king, who lay slumped in his chair.

'Boris,' called Hamish, a slight shudder running down his spine at having to speak to his tormentor. 'See to the king. Does he live?'

Boris rushed to his king's side and felt his face, then held his hand in front of the king's mouth.'

'He sleeps,' shouted Boris. 'Our king sleeps only. He is alive!'

'He what?' shouted Dudley. 'That witch has tricked me. But I have a few tricks myself.'

He closed his eyes and started humming, and the Great Hall grew darker and darker, as if night were falling. Many of the guards fell back, muttering in dismay at this sorcery. Then a faint rumbling could be heard, growing louder and louder.

'What is this?' shouted Mikka.

'Evil magic,' cried Hamish.

Lord Dudley clapped his hands together once, and the great doors started rattling, before shattering into tiny pieces, debris flying into the Hall. There was another enormous crash, and a hideous lair-goblin stood in the gaping hole where the doors had been, leering at Sir Hamish.

'Run! Fly! Run!' shouted the guards, dropping their weapons and fleeing the hall. The travelling players hid behind the great banquet table, a cloth drawn over their heads. Only Mikka, Boris, Hamish and Dudley stayed where they were. The champion spoke calmly to Mikka and Boris. 'Take cover,' he said. 'You cannot match this foe. He is mine.' Then he drew Justice from its scabbard and held the sword high over his head. He had no magic to help him this time, but he was still a great champion.

'Filthy creature from below!' shouted Hamish. 'Now you will die!'

Hamish rushed at the lair-goblin and swung his mighty sword hoping his skills with the blade would be enough.

Hamish stared up at the evil creature, panting heavily. His hand was trapped under Justice. The mighty sword had not been enough to defeat the creature, and now he was at its mercy. One thing he knew for sure, there would be precious little mercy shown. Dudley gave a slow hand-clap beside him, a wicked smile on his face.

'What a pity you don't have the Crystal Maiden to help you,' said Dudley. He knelt beside Hamish. 'Would you like my creature to kill you quickly?' he whispered. 'Or slowly, Hamish?'

The lair-goblin growled hungrily from above, drool dripping from its fangs.

'What does it matter?' said Hamish. 'I am done ...'

Whoa! Hold on a second, who said anything about dying. Come on, there's gotta be a way out ... Think! You defeated the troll, remember? And you survived all sorts of other dangers. Angry mobs, horrible smells, the landlord's bad breath ...

Beatrice ran into the Hall and rushed to Hamish's side. 'My love,' she cried, 'don't give up ...'

Lord Dudley roared with laughter, and the goblin joined in, its laugh a horrible hacking wheeze. 'Ah, it is the Crystal Maiden,' said Dudley. 'Do you want your bauble? I have the Crystal here ...' He pulled out a small glass bead and held it above Beatrice's head, taunting her with it. 'I will never give it back, you foolish wench.'

Beatrice stared hard at the crystal bauble in Dudley's hand. 'But,' she said, shaking her head, 'that thing ... it is not my Crystal.'

'It's not?' shouted Dudley.

Okay, here's a twist I didn't see coming. So if that's not the crystal, where the heck is the real thing?

Hamish closed his eyes, thinking back through his journey. There must be a clue in there somewhere. *Where is the crystal?* Suddenly he opened his eyes and smiled, reaching with his free hand into the pouch that hung round his neck. There was a lump in the stitching. He'd first felt it in the tavern. Ripping at the leather, Hamish released something cold and smooth from the pouch. A brilliant white light glowed from his hand.

Beatrice reached her hand out, tears streaking her cheek. 'You had it all along,' she whispered. 'My life, my light ... my Crystal.' She took the Crystal and held it aloft, filling the Hall with its magical light.

'But ... but,' stammered Dudley. 'If that is the Crystal, then what do I have here?'

'What you have,' whispered Hamish, 'is a teddy bear's eye.'

Dudley stared at Hamish blankly for a second, then shouted, 'Kill him!' to the lair-goblin.

The creature moved in for the final blow, but stopped as the Crystal Maiden stood, holding her powerful white light under its nose. The light radiated into every corner, and the horrible lair-goblin started to groan with pain, covering its eyes. Burn marks appeared on the thing's green hide, as if the light were frying it back to hell. The goblin screamed with misery, brushing at its skin with its razor-sharp claws. Eventually the pain grew too strong, and it released its foothold on Justice, turning to ward off the fierce maiden with the glowing Crystal who walked towards it.

Hamish stood in one smooth action, whipping the glass teddy bear eye from Dudley's grasp. 'I'll have that for Hitchcock,' he said. Then he wheeled around and completed the lunge he'd tried earlier, sinking Justice into the disgusting goblin. It squealed with shock, then fell with a crash to the floor.

Beatrice ran to Hamish, flinging her arms around his neck. 'Hamish, Hamish,' she cried. 'You won.'

He was about to answer her when a sharp cry rang out.

'Hamish! Look out!' shouted Zed.

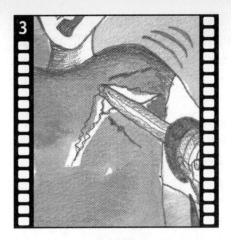

'No more!' cried Beatrice, holding her Crystal aloft.

Dudley paused, then smiled. Daggers were of no use against the Crystal Maiden. He closed his eyes and started his evil humming again, summoning some magic. The Crystal Maiden stepped between Dudley and Hamish, who was staring down in disbelief at the blood seeping through his tunic.

'Your magic is no match for mine,' Beatrice said.

'We shall see about that,' said Dudley.

A dark cloud filled the Hall, swirling around Beatrice's head, but she thrust the Crystal at it and the cloud melted into tiny drops of rain that burned holes into the carpet. Dudley bellowed with rage, then raised his hands high, his humming growing louder and louder. Once again the Hall grew dim. What evil magic was he calling now? Mikka and Boris, who had rushed to Hamish's aid, fell back, crippled with fear. The travelling players quaked in their hiding spot. The Hall fell into an evil, dank night. Dudley's arms quivered. He was about to clap his hands together to bring down his final magic when the pommel of Justice crashed down onto his head, knocking him senseless.

'No magic is a match for a good old knock to the head,' said Hamish.

The Hall burst into daylight again, and birds sang outside the windows. Guards rushed back in, cheering for the champion and the Crystal Maiden. The champion tried to raise Justice high, but he started swaying, Dudley's wound having taken its toll. As Dudley was dragged away to the dungeons by Boris, Beatrice led Hamish to a chair to tend to his wounds.

'Will you ever forgive me?' she whispered.

'As long as you forgive me for abandoning you,' said Hamish.

'I do,' smiled Beatrice.

'Then I do, too.'

Everyone gathered around to cheer their champion, and he stood shakily to oblige them. Beatrice flung her arms once more around Hamish's neck and he winced from the pain in his shoulder, yet still managed to smile.

From behind the cheering throng, a tired voice could be heard asking, 'What is all this cheering for?' They turned to see their king waking from his deep sleep.

'Hamish has saved the kingdom,' they cheered. 'Hamish the champion!'

25

Scene twenty–five

Beatrice was asleep in a chair next to Hamish's bed, having insisted that she stay up to tend to his wound. She had a smile on her lips, and her Crystal glowed with the soft light of contentment. Hamish woke. He'd had a strange dream about an even stranger land, where fast chariots flew along the roads, and flickering worlds could be seen everywhere.

What are you talking about? Chariots? Flickering worlds? They're cars and videos, dummy.

He shook his head, then touched Beatrice to see if she was real. Her skin still felt soft and smooth. *I'm completely back*, he thought. Hamish stretched, then winced with pain. Obviously wounds keep hurting for a long time in a Vidz. He crawled out of bed, then tiptoed out of the chamber to the antechamber, where Zed and Bee sat by the fire.

Elsewhere in the castle the king slept with an almighty headache, not helped by the news of his chief advisor's treachery. It had been the evidence of the head guard, Boris, that had convinced the king to keep Dudley in the prison. If Boris was prepared to give up the opportunity of torturing Hamish again, then the story of Dudley's treachery must be true. The king knew how much Boris liked his torture.

Hamish sat on the pile of rugs and furs, the pain in his shoulder biting as he twisted to get comfortable. An awful smell wafted past his nose from the herb poultice that Beatrice had put on his wound.

'What a fight,' said Bee, sighing contentedly.

'You were truly marvellous, Hamish,' said Zed.

He blushed, then scratched his head. 'I wasn't that good ...'

'How about that part where Dudley had the concealed dagger?' said Bee. 'I mean, talk about the corniest movie trick in the book ...'

His words trailed off as Zed shot him a desperate look. Bee went bright red himself, and mumbled something in a poor attempt to cover what he'd just said.

'What did you say?' asked Hamish.

'Nothing ... I ...'

'Did you say it was the corniest movie trick?' asked Hamish.

'Um ... yes,' said Bee.

'Mm,' said Hamish, deep in thought. 'You know, something has always bothered me about you two. Take last night, when we planned the Great Hall attack. You seemed to know all those moves I was talking about, like the falling candelabrum. It was as if you'd seen them before.'

'Well,' said Bee. 'We've played at so many castles ...'

'And yet you are young,' said Hamish.

'Young but full of experience,' said Zed.

Hamish scratched his chin, then he smiled. 'Did experience teach you to do a high five?'

The look on Zed and Bee's faces was priceless. Their mouths hung open and their eyes were as wide as saucers. The last thing they'd expected to hear was the people's champion using such a phrase.

Oh, if only I had a camera, thought Hamish. *This would make a great shot.*

'How did you ...?' began Bee.

'He means, how could you ...?' added Zed.

'Know about high fives?' asked Hamish. 'Because I'm from the same place you two probably are.'

'Capra?' said Bee.

Hamish nodded. Zed gasped, but Bee slapped his knee and shouted, 'I told you, didn't I? I told you he wasn't a real swordsman. I knew it.'

'Who are you?' whispered Zed.

'I'm Hamish,' said Hamish. 'Although I think I've mostly been Sir Hamish for the past day or so. It's so totally weird. It's like I've been ... completely inside the character ...'

'The character?' said Bee.

'Then ... you don't really look like that?' asked Zed.

'No ... I look like ... um ... like Hamish.'

'Hamish?' shrieked Zed. 'Not that kid who was fiddling around with the lockers?'

'I wasn't fiddling around,' said Hamish, blushing again. The painful memory of his life at Capra came flooding back to him. It was too much to bear after the magnificent time he'd had being Hamish the Great, the people's champion. 'I am that lonely kid at Capra Video School, but I'm *not* a thief. And you two are ...?'

'I'm Kaz,' said Zed.

'And I'm Bo,' said Bee.

'Two of the three remaining Vidz directors,' said Hamish, the realisation suddenly dawning on him.

'The ... what?'

Hamish told them about First Director, and receiving his Vidz, and how he was thrown into this movie to fight evil, and how evil had a mirror in real life, and that was why it was so important to defeat Dudley. Kaz and Bo listened intently, asking questions now and then, but mostly nodding their heads. When Hamish had finished they sat silent for a while, taking it all in.

Eventually Bo said, 'There's something else that's pretty weird. Kaz had one of those Vidz thingies at her place ...'

'You did?' said Hamish. Now it was his turn to be shocked. 'The Vidz must have realised I needed help, and sent you two in ...'

'You know,' said Kaz, standing and pacing the room, 'this is kinda crazy and spooky, just between you and me. I can handle it if this is a dream, but videos that fly to my home so I'll watch them and then go into their world. I mean ... really!'

Hamish started laughing, and Bo joined in too. Kaz glared at them for a few seconds, then she too started giggling. 'I guess this is pretty real,' she said. 'That is, unless it's still a dream.'

'I doubt if three people can have the same dream,' said Hamish. 'You're here because of the Vidz. It's put you here to start your new life off ... as Vidz directors. That's what Michael told me. Either I'd find you, or you'd find me. Looks like you came to me.'

Bo looked at Hamish and grinned. 'I knew you weren't the real article,' he said.

'How?' asked Hamish. 'I look like a young man. I mean, when I really look hard at you two, you look like Kaz and Bo.'

'It was when you said something about a flash, back in that hut. No swordsman would know anything about a flash.'

'And you kept quiet all this time?'

'Are you kidding?' said Kaz. 'We'd just been saved from becoming some troll's lunchmeat. I mean, all we wanted to do was keep our heads, you know?'

'Of course,' said Hamish.

They laughed as they remembered how the troll had burst into the hut with takeaway dinner under each arm. It had been scary at the time, but now it was pretty funny. Each of them took turns to recount their favourite part of the adventure, then their scariest part, then their funniest part. It was a living, laughing, lively movie review in the middle of the movie!

'What do we do now? asked Bo. 'How do we get back?'

'Easy,' said Hamish. 'You just yell, "Cut".'

'That's it?' said Kaz. 'Wish I'd known that a while ago.'

'But then you wouldn't have been able to have this journey with me,' said Hamish.

'Okay,' said Bo, holding his hand out to Hamish. 'I'm ready. Let's do it.'

'You two go,' said Hamish, twisting his hands on his lap.

'What are you going to do?' asked Kaz.

'I'll stay ...'

'To say goodbye?'

'No ... I'll stay for good,' said Hamish.

'You'll what?' shrieked Bo. 'Are you out of your mind? You're a Capra student, not a champion. You belong home with us.'

'Do I?' shouted Hamish. 'I'm that strange, lonely kid, remember? I'm the one who no-one talks to. I'm the one who everyone thinks is a thief. At least here I learned about working together with someone. I'm loved, and I have a place ...'

'Hamish,' said Kaz in a gentle voice. 'This is a movie. It's not real.'

'Look around you,' said Hamish. 'Feels pretty real to me.'

Bo stood up and paced around the room. 'Oh, man,' he said. 'You're just ... I don't know ... stubborn. Just because you wrote that stuff in your essay about wanting to live in a movie ... it's nuts. Come with us.'

'No!' Hamish winced with pain, the wound in his

shoulder stinging badly. 'No. I have a chance to be happy here ...'

'That's rubbish!' shouted Kaz, standing with Bo. 'You could be happy at Capra if you tried.'

'I have no friends ...'

'What do you think we are?' said Bo. 'We like you.'

'You think I'm a thief.'

'Hey,' said Kaz. 'I'm sorry about that. We can talk about it ...'

Hamish shook his head. 'Please don't make this any harder than it is. Just go.'

'But you talked about working together,' said Bo. 'Well, we're the Vidz team, aren't we? We have a job to do ...'

'Sorry,' said Hamish. 'You two find another First Director.'

'Come on, Bo,' said Kaz. 'This is a waste of time. You ready?'

Bo nodded his head. 'I'm ready.'

They both turned to Hamish. 'Come back,' said Kaz. Then they shouted, 'Cut!' and were gone.

Hamish felt an intense sadness at their departure, and he tried to shake it off with a quick shrug. Why should he be sad? He was Sir Hamish here in this land ... this movie. The king liked him again, and tomorrow he'd give him gold, and land, and happiness.

Hamish wandered into the bedchamber. *I must remember to ask for a horse from the king as well*, he thought. He'd have more than he could ever hope for here, more than at Capra Video High School.

He sat on the end of the bed, trying to keep up his

enthusiasm for his new life. Somehow it didn't seem as wonderful and enticing as it had before. He couldn't shake off what Kaz and Bo had said to him. They liked him. They wanted him to come back. And now they were a team, just as Sir Hamish and the Crystal Maiden had been a team.

Beatrice was still asleep in the chair, and Hamish decided to climb into bed and make a decision in the morning. He was about to pull back the covers when he noticed that someone was already in the bed. It was a man, gently snoring. He tried to feel angry, outraged, but all he could muster was curiosity. It was as if he was slowly fading away from this world.

Hamish took a candle and peered at the stranger as he slept, holding the flame up so he could see the man's face. It was Sir Hamish, the people's champion. A handsome young man, with a thin scar on his cheek, and another forming now on his shoulder.

'I didn't look half bad,' muttered Hamish. He stood looking at his old self for a while, then whispered, 'Good night.' Hamish crept around to Beatrice, placed the candle back in its holder and gave the lady a kiss on her cheek.

'Good night, Beatrice,' he whispered. 'You were held by an evil bargain once, but in the end you helped me.  Now all will be well in a land you could only ever dream about. Goodbye.' Then he stood back and said, 'Cut!'

26

Scene twenty–six

The minute Hamish returned to his bedroom he noticed two things at once. He no longer felt as strong as he had, and the wound in his shoulder was just a dull ache that he remembered getting when he fell into the window of the girls' toilets.

Which was my first act of heroism, he thought.

He was back in his old life again, living with Aunt Jenny, eating alone at lunchtime, defending his innocence at Capra. He could hear the sound of the TV from the other room, and peered in at Aunt Jenny. She was still watching the same movie that she started way back when Hamish was doing the dishes. Since then he'd been to the car park and returned home to enter *A Dangerous Secret* again. But no time had passed in the real world. He'd trekked for days to a castle and fought a terrifying battle, and his world hadn't altered one bit.

Except, maybe, that evil is weaker now, he thought.

The phone rang, and Hamish jumped.

'Get that, would you, Hame?' said Aunt Jenny.

She hasn't even noticed that I've gone anywhere. He picked up the receiver, amazed at how ordinary this world seemed to him now.

'Hello,' he said.

'Is that the people's champion?' came a voice.

Hamish froze, until he realised it was Kaz. She laughed down the phone, saying she knew he'd come back. They'd only just returned, and wanted to come to his place straight away. Hamish asked Aunt Jenny if it was okay if some friends came over for a while, and she 'ummed' for a second or two, then said it would be 'lovely' if he had some friends over.

Kaz said she had Hamish's address from the class list. He hung up and went to his room, picking up Hitchcock and pulling the glass eye from his pocket. 'I'll sew this on for you tomorrow, Hitch. Okay?'

The bear did not answer.

Hamish sat on his bed, feeling nervous. What would he say to Kaz and Bo in this world? Then he realised: he was Hamish Wajda, First Director and leader of a team. He had lots to say to them. After a few minutes there was a knock at the front door, and Hamish got up to let the other Vidz directors in.

'We've only got half an hour,' said Kaz. 'Then my dad will pick us up. He's gone to the all-night supermarket.'

'All-night supermarket,' muttered Hamish, shaking his head. He led them to his bedroom. 'Does this world seem strange now?' he asked.

Bo laughed and said it was weird that your own world should seem weird! Kaz showed Hamish the Vidz that had been at her place. It now had gold lettering: 'Kaz Murneau, Second Director.' Hamish dug under his bed and pulled out the envelope with the other two Vidz in it. Sure enough, one had the words, 'Bo Griffiths, Third Director,' on it. The fourth was still blank.

'No Fourth Director yet,' said Hamish.

'I wonder who it is?' said Kaz.

'Don't know,' said Hamish. 'But I guess we'll discover the same way I discovered you two. No doubt your Vidz will show different movies when it's time for you to be the heroes. We're the Vidz team, we fight evil in the movies ... and here too. Only, I don't know what's evil here. There's no Dudleys with black cowls and horrible sneers ...'

'Yes there is,' said Kaz. 'Cushing.'

'Cushing?' said Hamish. 'Is he really that evil? I mean, I know he hates you, and probably tried to frame you for stealing a camera ...'

'He what?' shrieked Kaz.

Hamish quickly told her the true story about the lockers, and she shook her head slowly, apologising to him for thinking he may have been the thief.

'You'd better tell him about you and Cushing,' said Bo. 'I mean, we've fought off trolls and goblins together. I reckon you can trust him.'

'Okay,' said Kaz. 'Firstly, Cushing used to be my dad's business partner, but the business went bad. Cushing blames my dad, but we think that Cushing was actually taking money from the business for gambling. It all ended up horribly, and Cushing hates my family. So, when I turned up at Capra, he sees me, I see him, and from that day he's tried to make my life miserable.'

'But that's not real evil,' said Hamish. 'I mean, that's no mirror to what Dudley did.'

'No, there's more,' said Kaz. 'Cushing has taken money from the school. Lots of it. Probably to gamble again. And he's got some kind of hold over Arbuckle ...'

Kaz went on to tell Hamish about the strange conversation she and Bo had witnessed. Once she'd finished the room went quiet.

'Dudley and Ronald, Cushing and Arbuckle,' said Hamish after a pause. 'So, the Vidz really does mirror real life.'

'How do we defeat Cushing? We don't have a Crystal Maiden here,' said Bo.

'No,' said Hamish.

There was a knock at the door, and Aunt Jenny came in to say Kaz's dad had arrived.

'Okay,' Kaz said. Then she turned to Hamish. 'Tomorrow at school, we plan how we get Cushing. Tonight we think about it. All right?'

'All right,' said Hamish.

They left him alone on the bed, deep in thought. He hadn't felt this excited since he'd found out he got into Capra. It was just as the old First Director had said: this was going to be some ride.

Scene twenty–seven

Kaz wanted to march in on Cushing and say she knew what he was up to and how he was blackmailing the Principal, but Hamish reminded her of what had happened to Sir Hamish the first time he did that.

'You need proof,' he said.

Crouching outside Mr Arbuckle's window with a tape-recorder all week was hardly going to work, so they had to come up with something different. It was Bo who thought of the first good idea.

'Dudley thought Beatrice was poisoning the wine, right? She did what he asked, only she really made a sleeping spell. Cushing wants more money from Arbuckle. So, why don't we give it to him?'

'What?' Kaz had shrieked. 'How can we do that?'

'We don't,' Bo answered. 'But we make Cushing believe that Arbuckle wants to give him more money, just like Dudley believed that Beatrice poisoned the wine.'

And that was how Vidz directors numbers one, two and three wound up at the dog track standing in the betting ring.

Hamish wore an old overcoat from the costume wardrobe at Capra, a scratchy, stiff woollen thing that reminded him of the washerwoman disguise. Underneath he had a concealed digicam, ready to capture a bit of evidence. Earlier that day he'd left a fake note that Mr Arbuckle had supposedly written in Cushing's pigeonhole, asking Cushing to meet him at the dog track. As soon as the bursar arrived, the team went into action. Hamish at the betting ring, Bo nearby, and Kaz hiding next to the kiosk with a secret weapon that would be used near the end.

Their plan relied on Cushing's weakness. Would he have a bet at the track while he waited for Arbuckle? And would it be a big enough bet to prove that he'd used the school's money? A hundred dollars wouldn't do. But a thousand would be proof, because Cushing was a man in debt, he'd just come from a bankrupt business with Kaz's dad. There was no way he could have that much money, unless it wasn't his own.

Cushing seemed nervous as he stood in the ring, looking around for Arbuckle. The first race came and went but he didn't bet. The second race was run, and still no bet. Hamish was beginning to think the plan was a fizzer when Cushing approached a bookmaker to place a bet on a horse. Hamish pressed the *record* button, stood nearby and started shooting.

'How much?' asked the bookie's scribe.

Cushing felt in his pocket and pulled out a huge wad of money. 'Twenty thousand on three,' said Cushing, looking over his shoulder.

The scribe wrote out the bet as Cushing spotted Hamish with the overcoat and concealed camera.

'What are you doing?' shouted the bursar, advancing on Hamish.

That's when Bo sprang into action. He rushed up to Cushing and took his hand, yelling, 'Please, Dad, come home. Mum hasn't got any food in the house. We need you. Please come home, Daddy ...'

He repeated this performance over and over as a small crowd gathered around, shaking their heads. The scribe held up the bet, saying, 'What'll I do with this?', and Kaz took it from him, handing it to Cushing.

'This is your bet,' she said. 'But it wasn't your money.'

'You won't get away with this,' shouted Cushing.

'Oh yes we will,' smiled Kaz, and she produced her secret weapon.

Bright lights flashed in Cushing's eyes, causing him to cry out with pain. When the horrible spots from the flashes had vanished, he saw that a newspaper photographer was grinning at him, saying, 'Thanks for the shots.' He was no maiden, but his 'crystal' was bright enough.

The Vidz team had gathered enough evidence to rid the school of Cushing. The newspaper the next day carried a photo of the bursar with the headline, 'Bankrupt

Businessman Bets Thousands!' Hamish handed the secret videotape over to Arbuckle, saying the Principal could do what he liked with it.

Arbuckle glared at Hamish, and tried to say he had no idea what Cushing was doing betting large amounts of money. But he still kept the tape, and he hurried Hamish out of his office, slamming the door behind him. Something wasn't right about Arbuckle, but Hamish knew there was nothing he could do about it for now.

As they gathered at school the next day, reading the newspaper story about Cushing, the Vidz crew felt the satisfaction of having beaten an enemy by working together.

'Hey, have you heard? Cushing's been fired. He's gone!'

'I could get used to beating the bad guy ...'

Hamish: 'Why zero?'
Teacher: 'You handed it in late ...'

'Looks as if Dudley... I mean Cushing,
wounded me after all.'

Fade out ...

Stay tuned for the next thrilling episode of Vidz: *Time Trap!*

What's the point of being a Vidz director and saving the world when your personal life is going down the drain?

Kaz wants to remain the most popular girl in her year, but how is she going to do that when she can't even buy herself a soft drink? Ever since her dad's business went broke, everything has gone wrong. If only she could go back in time and change everything so she still had money. But that sort of thing only happens in movies, right? Or ... in a Vidz!

Vidz number two. Coming soon!

About the author

Ian Bone began writing books for young people in 1993, and has had over 25 titles published, including *The Song of an Innocent Bystander*, *That Dolphin Thing*, *Tin Soldiers* (shortlisted in the 2001 NSW Premier's Awards) and *Fat Boy Saves World*. His books have been published in the USA, UK, Korea and Germany, and six of his titles have been listed as Notable Books by the Children's Book Council of Australia.

Just like his *Vidz* characters, Ian Bone loves movies, has studied film history, and knows way too much about strange and obscure films. Ian has always wanted to create a book that would combine great storytelling with video techniques. When he was awarded the Carclew Fellowship in 2000, he used the time to develop the *Vidz* series. He says there's a little bit of himself in each of the *Vidz* characters. He still gets a thrill when the lights go down in the cinema and the main feature begins. And yes, when he was young, he wished he could live his life in a movie.

Ian lives in Adelaide and is currently writing more titles in the *Vidz* series.

About the illustrator

Jobi Murphy is a freelance designer and illustrator who has worked on numerous books for Random House including *Muddled Up Farm*, *Max Remy: Superspy*, *The Saddle Club*, *Pony Tails* and the *Vidz* series. She was also responsible for designing Blake Education's award-winning *My Alphabet Kit*.

Despite being discouraged from mixing her colours by her second-grade teacher, Jobi fulfilled a long-time ambition when she began working in children's publishing. She now divides her time between illustrating and designing children's books, and enjoying time with her husband and baby son in the bushy Sydney suburb of Grays Point.